Chapter 1

I0557087

It was about two hours past midday and Matthew Patterson was leading his two horses upstream along the Ouachita river. He held his white mare with a short rope and his bay gelding with a ten foot rope because the bank was steep and the way was narrow. Up ahead he saw that the bank was much lower and there was a fairly large clear area covered with sumac and henbit. When he got there he stopped and let his animals graze. There were enough hoof prints and wagon tracks in the area that he could tell that this spot was where flatboats were used to cross the river and horses were swum across. That would have been when the river was lower and the current not as swift. Right now it was quite swollen with the spring runoff. He imagined a rope-tow ferry in this location. Since he had left Ireland eight months before he had been looking for a spot like this. In the distance he could hear and smell the sounds of civilization. After letting his animals graze for a few minutes, he gathered up his lead ropes and walked west, up the riverbank, towards the town. The path was a little wider than a four-wheeled wagon and overhung with oak and sweet gum trees. Tree roots crisscrossed the path. After fifty yards the ground leveled out. There were frame buildings on both sides of the path and a large, white building beside a huge oak tree lay straight ahead. The smell of horse manure told him he was near a livery stable. The stable was on his right as he drew closer. There was a very large black man just outside the corral pounding on an anvil. Matthew was well over six feet in height and weighed over two hundred pounds. His hair was red and curly and and his booted feet were size nine. The other man was shorter, but outweighed Matthew by fifty pounds. Very soon a small boy appeared from the barn and trotted over to where Matthew was standing.

"Want me to take care of them horses, sir?" the boy asked.

"Why certainly, laddie. Pull those packs from their backs and let them have a rest. What's your name, lad?"

"Jimmy Sykes, sir. You go 'head over and talk to Mr. Ira."

"That I will, lad, yes indeed." By then Ira had left his anvil. and was walking towards him. "Matthew Patterson, sir," he extended his hand.

"My name's Ira," he replied, taking Matthew's hand.

They sat on a bench by the stable door. After fishing in his pocket for a penny for Jimmy, he asked Ira if he knew the folks thereabout. Ira said, "I know most of 'ems horses better, but I knows the people too."

"What do they call this town, Ira?"

"This is West Creek, Arkansas, an' it's in Union County." His voice dropped a little. "Gen'l Grant led the U.S. Army and whupped the Confed'ret Army. So they made this county for the folks on the U.S. Side. But most the folks here ain't."

"I see, but are there any folks here from the U.S. Side?"

"Only ones I know is Maj. Jim Thornton's family. They live out on Darley Hill, west of town. Mr. Matthew, do you believe in drinkin' wine?"

"Yes, I do, Mr. Ira, if there's any to be found." Ira left him hanging on that word while he motioned him over to the shade of an oak tree beside the stable. Matthew followed him and reached out to take the earthenware jug that Ira handed him. He pulled the cork and took a draft of the wine. He handed the jug back to Ira, who also took a drink.

"This muscadine wine from right here in this valley. If you ever needs any you can always get it from me."

"Ira, do you have any oats or corn I can feed my horses?"

"Sho do," Ira replied, "I got corn."

"Would you give them each two pounds of corn while I stroll toward the town square?"

"Yes, suh, I will."

Matthew shook the blacksmith's hand and walked toward the largest building in sight. It was the town's hotel, and he saw a young man who appeared to be examining an assortment of pieces of lumber. He was almost as tall as Matthew, with dark hair and a slighter build.

"Good day, sir," Matthew said, "I'm Matthew Patterson, I'm new in town."

"I'm Mitchell Hendricks, I'm fairly new in town, myself. I'm staying at the Methodist Church with Rev. Davis. I'm trying to build a porch on this hotel. Judge Jacobs wants a porch here, and I told him if he provided me the lumber I would do the best I could to supply. Have you got any talent for carpentry?"

"Well, I've been known to. If you have nails, and a hammer,

and a saw, and some string, that's all we need. Are you offering me part of your enterprise?"

"I told the judge I'd find another boy to help me. Whatever he pays we'll split, plus we'll eat whatever Miss Clothilda cooks in the hotel kitchen."

"Can Miss Clothilda cook?"

"She can cook anything the Lord provides and makes it taste better than manna. She's a Creole lady from New Orleans."

"I've just come from New Orleans and I love Creole food. Mitchell, you've got yourself a deal."

"In that case, let's go inside and see what Miss Clothilda has in the kitchen."

Clothilda was a slightly heavy-set brown-skinned woman. She wore a long cotton dress with a white apron and she was setting dishes and silverware on the table. It was a large oval table in the middle of the dining room, where a middle-aged man was sitting and reading a folded-over paper. As Mitch and Matthew entered the room he rose and introduced himself. "I am Seth Tate, gentlemen."

"I'm Matthew Patterson and this is my compatriot, Mitchell Hendricks."

"Happy to meet you both."

Clothilda set a bowl of red kidney beans and a bowl of rice on the table. "Y'all help yourselves, I'll get the corn bread and sweet 'taters."

When she returned from the kitchen, Matthew spoke, "You're from New Orleans, ma'am?"

She sat down at the table and smiled. "Yes, lived there all my life until Judge Jacobs hired me to come here and cook for the hotel. My name is Clothilda Marie Bechet, and my family is Creole French." She didn't have to ask if the men liked the food, they all dived in with obvious pleasure.

"I have in mind to start a ferry on the river, and I would need to pitch a tent on the bank. Who would I speak to about my plans?" Matthew asked.

"The judge is the man to talk to," Mitchell replied, "We need to go see him after we finish eating, you can talk to him then."

Chapter 2

"Ah, Mitchell," Judge Jacobs said, I see you've brought a friend. What does he have to say?"

"Matthew Patterson, guv'ner," Matthew began, offering his large right hand, I've been offered a position of helping Mitchell build a porch. That's the current business. And I want to tell you that I plan to operate a ferry on the river. With your permission I'd like to pitch my tent on the riverbank."

The judge motioned them to chairs in the front room. "Well, Matthew, why don't you proceed with your plans for the time being. I don't know anything about you except I assume that you're Irish."

"Yes, sir, I am. Since I left Cork, my plan has been to make a ferry upstream from the Mississippi. West Creek seems to be as good a place as any."

The judge nodded, "The local population are simple folk. Now, if you were brought up Catholic, I would advise you not to make that well known.
These people may have been told things that need not be brought forth, if you know what I mean."

"Yes, sir, I believe I do. One reason I came here was to leave behind the constant quarrels with the British."

Mitchell added, "I won't say anything about it. You're welcome to come to Reverend Davis' church with me, which would be taken by local folks that your beliefs are like most of theirs."

"A good idea, Matthew replied.

"Now boys, finish your hammering around suppertime. Folks will appreciate the quiet. Just like everything else, don't give folks a reason to get upset and we'll all be better off."

Their business with the judge over, Mitchell and Matthew rose. The judge followed them to the door. As they were leaving Judge Jacobs' house, a tall man riding a black horse approached from the west.

"Good evening Major," the judge said, "Boys, I'd like you to meet Maj. Thornton. Major, this is Mitchell Hendricks and Matthew Patterson. I'm hoping they will be long-time residents of our community."

"Nice to make your acquaintance, gentlemen. Judge, could

I have a moment of your time?"

Matthew and Mitchell returned to their building project. Judge Jacobs invited the major in.

"What can I do for you, Jim?"

"There's a boy that's been helping the blacksmith, his name is Jimmy. I'm interested in having him work for me. I hoped you might be able to tell me what approach to use."

"I know the boy you mean. Let me give you the background on his family. Jimmy, I believe his last name is Sykes, lives with Pearlie White in what is known as the Yellow House, which she owns. She is the guardian of a number of colored orphans. She does work for several white families, as do a couple of her girls. I think she may be happy to have Jimmy work for you, if he wants to. I would suggest you call on her and make your proposal. Miss Pearl has a certain status in this town. Only she knows the kinship of all these children. She gets a little income from anonymous sources, and as far as I'm concerned, if she can raise these children to be responsible adults, she's got my support."

"Very interesting," the major said, nodding his head. "What would be an acceptable amount to pay him, if he stays at my farm during the week?"

"Oh, room and board and ten cents a day would be sufficient."

"That was the figure I had in mind," Maj. Thornton replied.

Judge Jacobs offered Maj. Thornton a glass of tea. Miss Finchley, the judge's housekeeper, brought the tea. They continued talking about Miss Pearl and her children. The judge said that he found it interesting that the children had last names but not all the same last name.

"I believe Pearlie can identify the parents of all of them, but it's better to leave that up to her and not interfere."

Several days later Maj. Thornton rode over to the Yellow House. As he approached the house, three small dark faces appeared in the front window. Within seconds Jimmy emerged from the house.

"Eve'nin' Major Thornton, want me to tend to yo' horse?"

"Just tie a rein to a rock and come inside, I need to talk to Miss Pearl."

The major waited while Jimmy came back and opened the door.

"Mama, Maj. Thornton want to talk to you."

His mother was standing in the small front room surrounded by two small boys, a small girl, and a teen-aged girl.

"Jimmy, introduce us to the Major."

"Yes, ma'am, Major, this is my mama Pearl White, my sister, Ivory White, my sister Essie Mary White, and my brothers, Wendell and Tyndall Sykes. And he is Maj. Thornton. Mr. Ira takes care of his horses."

"Won't you sit down, Major," Pearl offered. The major took one of two chairs, the two girls sat on a small bench, and Jimmy and the twin boys sat on the floor.

Maj. Thornton wasn't quite sure how to begin the conversation. He just kept it simple, "You have a lovely family, Miss Pearl."

"Thank you, sir."

"I would like to offer Jimmy a job, ma'am. He would work with my horses. He would stay at my house Monday through Friday and come home on Saturday and Sunday. He'd eat with us and have his own bed and I'll provide him with some clothing. I would pay him ten cents a day to start with."

"That sounds very nice to me, sir. Jimmy, would you like to do that?"

Jimmy couldn't help smiling, "Yes, ma'am, I would."

"In that case," said the major, "I'll come by for you day after tomorrow. I was called 'Jimmy' as a child. Now I'm known as 'Jim' to my family. Why don't we call you, 'Little Jim' and I'll be 'Big Jim'?"

"That's fine with me," answered the boy.

"You'll like the folks at Darley Hill," the major continued, "The cook will prepare meals three time a day. You'll need to have boots to wear while you're riding and I'll take care of that. How does that sound so far?"

"Very good, sir," Jimmy replied.

"Well, Miss Pearl, you have a lovely family. Your boy won't be far away and we'll take good care of him. Feel free to get in touch with us any time you need to. I"ll say goodbye for now and I'll see you day after tomorrow."

Chapter 3

After Big Jim left, the twins had many questions for their brother. "What you gonna do at yo' job?" Tyndall asked. "He got these horses. Not reg'lar horses, they race horses. When you race horses, you got to have a small man, 'cause a big man would slow the horse down," Little Jim replied.

"How you know so much about race horses?" asked Ivory.

"Ira tol' me all about it."

Ivory sighed, "Please be careful, Jimmy. Them horses so big and you so little."

"But you see, Ira always say, we don't make 'em do anything. They want to do what we want 'em to do, and they trust us."

"Well make sure they trustin' you, 'cause we care about you."

Pearl said, "Little Jim, that's what we gone call you now, Ira says you know somethin' about horses most folks never know. I think that's why Big Jim wants you workin' for him. Right now y'all need to help me, 'cause I got to fix supper."

Little Jim went to the well for a bucket of water. Wendell and Tyndall stood behind him holding onto his waist while he lowered the bucket. He weighed just over eighty pounds, and it was a lot easier to pull up the bucket if he had help. The boys didn't have shoes to wear. Pearl had a pair of shoes she had bought from a catalogue that belonged to a white family she worked for. Ivory also had a pair that were given to her by another white family that she had done some work for. Essie Mary, like the boys, didn't have shoes. For Jimmy to have a pair of boots made for him was highly unusual in a place like Union County.

When the boys had returned with the water, Essie and Ivory were shelling peas. Pearl said to Jimmy, "The Major didn't say you was gonna be a jockey, but I guess that's what you'll be. Twins, what are y'all gonna do before supper?"

"Mama, we're makin' a big 'ol fishin' pole. Big enough so we can catch the biggest catfish in the river."

"Well don't you be botherin' the big red-haired man down there, he's buildin' a ferry and he don't need you in his way."

"Oh that's Mr. Patterson. He's our friend, but we won't be gettin' in his way."

Wendell and Tyndall had an eight foot long hickory pole

which was two inches in diameter at the base. The hook was large enough for the heaviest fish they might catch and the line was heavy cotton twine. The whole rig was way too heavy for the pan fish they usually fished for, but they were planning for the largest catfish they might encounter. The level of the river was fairly high because it was spring. Later in the year they sometimes dived for mussels, when the water level was lower and the current wasn't so swift. But this time of year cat fishing was their main agenda.

For their supper they had field peas, turnip greens, and hush puppies. After Pearl had asked the blessing they started eating.

"Mama, is these puppies made with the hominy grits?" Tyndall asked.

"Baby, that's what they is. When I was at Miz Biggs' house she told me how Doctor Biggs says it's the best way to do corn. He says all the Indians did it this way and they never had no skin trouble and never got sick. So that's what I'll be doin' with the corn from now on."

"I like the hush puppies, Mama." The other children sounded their agreement.

After their supper, Wendell and Tyndall took their new pole out in the yard. Wendell laid one end of it on his shoulder; his brother laid the other end on his shoulder, and, side-by-side, they walked the path down to the riverbank. Matthew and Mitchell were in the process of building a flatboat, which would become the ferry. Having told their mother that they wouldn't bother Matthew, they waved at him upon their arrival and set about preparing their line. They had tied a rock, which weighed about a quarter pound, close to the end of their line. The hook was baited with a whole chicken gizzard. The line was about fifteen feet. The laid the pole on the bank, with the big end close to the water and the small end perpendicular to the stream. The line was laid back from the small end. They both took hold of the pole about five feet from the big end. Tyndall put one foot in front of the big end, and together they raised the pole in a sweeping motion that launched the line well out into the water. Then they both sat down on the pole to await action form the denizens of the Ouachita.

Matthew's plan was to apply tar to all the seams between the boards on his flatboat. It would be large enough to carry two horses at a time. Perhaps in the future he might get a bigger boat that could carry a wagon and two horses all at once, but for now the wagon would have to cross separately from the horses. Once the craft had been built and tarred, he would paint it with four or five layers of oil paint so it would hold up for a long time. The ferry would be powered by horses. A wheel-like device, the size of a well house, would provide the mechanical advantage so that a continuous rope could be pulled by one horse. Walking in a circle around the wheel, the boat could be towed back and forth across the river.

At about six o'clock Matthew and Mitchell laid down their tools and walked over to the hotel for their supper. The Sykes boys had had their line in the water for three quarters of an hour. "Come on big catfish, smell that gizzard. Don't it smell good?" Tyndall called out.

"He smellin' it," Wendell said, "he gotta taste it befo' we catch him. Sun goin' down, he oughta be gettin' hungry." They patiently talked to their prey while they sat on their pole as the Sun dipped lower in the sky.

A short time later Matthew came walking back to his ferry site. Mitch had gone back to the parsonage for evening. Very soon the Sykes boys felt their rig twitching and they knew their patience would soon be rewarded. They got all four of their hands around the pole and kept the line taut. But it soon became apparent that the fish they had hooked was more than their combined strengths could manage. Matthew quickly noticed their struggle and came to their aid. Both boys had arm and hand holds on the pole, and Matthew got behind them and added his two massive hands to the rig. With the line jerking back and forth in the water, Matthew backed away from the bank, taking the boys, the pole, and the fish with him. As they dragged their catch out of the river, they could see it was a catfish in excess of twelve pounds as it flopped up and down on the riverbank.

"We got 'im, we got 'im," both boys screamed at the top of their lungs. They were laughing and crying at the same time and Matthew was laughing with them.

Matthew helped them wind the line around the middle of the pole, so with an end of the pole on each boys shoulder, they were able to carry it, albeit with the tail of the fish dragging the ground. They marched triumphantly up the trail to the big oak and south to the Yellow House, singing, "We caught a big fish, we caught a big fish." A few of the townspeople were sitting on their porches and witnessed the procession.

Remarks were made, "Did you see that catfish them little niggers was carryin'?"

Chapter 4

Major Thornton arrived at the Yellow House just as Miss Pearl's family was finishing breakfast. Jimmy had packed both of his shirts and both pairs of pants into a cotton sack. He had no underwear or shoes or socks. He had a few prized possessions which he left in the care of his family; a few arrowheads, a few beads from river clams, a wooden gun. His brothers could play with them during the week when he was at the Major's house. He knew he could trust them for their safe-keeping.

He gave his mama and his sisters a goodbye embrace. Pearl couldn't help feeling a bit sentimental. He was her first to be gone from home, even though he would not be far away and would be home two days a week. Big Jim had driven down in the buck board, pulled by his tall chestnut harness horse. Finally they were on their way, driving through the middle of town and out the road to the west. Half a mile out of town they stopped at the home of Jacob "Gunner Jake" Miles.

Jake owned an artillery piece, a relic of the Civil War. On the Fourth of July and other special occasions he would fire it in the direction of the river. He never loaded it with a projectile, one never knew if there was a flaw in the casting that might finally fail with the pressure of an explosion.

Jake was also a capable boot-maker. He was sitting on his front porch when Big Jim and his new rider approached. "Good morning Mr. Thornton, how are you sir?" he said.

"Very fine, thank-you. This is my new hired hand, Little Jim Sykes. He will be riding my horses and he needs a good pair of boots."

Jake had him stand on the edge of the porch while he used a pencil to make an outline of Jimmy's feet. "How tall should these boots be," he asked.

"Just below his knee," the Major replied.

Jake directed, "Sit down, boy, and stretch out your leg." Jake drew a line from Jimmy's foot to below his knee to use as a pattern. "I'd say about a week, Mr. Thornton."

"That's fine, Jake." The major replied.

Little Jim got back in the buckboard and they headed southwest toward Darley Hill.

"How come he don't call you Major, sir?" Jimmy asked.

"Well, he fought in the Confederate army, so I'm not his comrade in arms. But he treats me right and that's good enough for me," was the major's reply.

"Your boots won't be ready this week, so we'll get you acquainted with the rest of my staff and family- and show you around Darley Hill."

"How come it's Darley Hill?" Jimmy asked.

"See, these race horses are called thoroughbreds. Their bloodlines go back to a few great horses who came from the old country across the sea. Horses like the Godolphin Arabian, the Darley Arabian, the Curwen Bay Barb, and the Byerley Turk. My horses are descended from the Darley Arabian, the greatest of them all. So I named my farm Darley Hill."

"Oh, so their mamas and daddies was famous before they come to America?"

"That's right. They won races back in England and we hope they'll win races here. My three-year-old is named Cardinal Archbishop, but we call him Redbird, for short. Do you like horses that can run?"

"I guess I do, Mr. Ira always told me to hold 'em back and not let 'em run, but I always wanted to turn 'em loose and run as fast as they can."

"Well Jim, what's right at the heart of this business is to know when to hold them back, and when to let them run, and I think you're the kind of boy that can do just that."

"I'm gonna try the best I can, sir."

"I believe you will, son, I believe you will."

The staff were all standing on the front porch as Big Jim drove under the archway onto the farm road. "Does that say 'Darley Hill', sir?" Jimmy inquired.

"Yes it does, can you read, son?"

"No, sir, but Miss Pearl been teachin' me."

"Well, we'll work on that, we'll have you reading before we're through."

Major Thornton stopped the horse in front of the porch and Jimmy jumped down from the buck board. "Little Jim, this is Chester, he's in charge of the stable and all the horses." Jimmy shook his hand. "Chester, will you drive the buck board to the stable and take care of Dancer."

"Yes, sir. Fine lookin' boy sir."

"Mattie is our cook, Brooks is our butler, Anna Lee, and Chara Kee are our housekeepers."

Jimmy shook hands with each of them.

Mattie said, "Dinner will be ready soon. Little Jim, go with the girls to the wash basin then come to the table. We're having chicken and dumplings."

"Yes, ma'am. Which one 'o you is Chara and which one is Anna?"

"I'm Chara and I'm taller and I'm darker." said Chara."

"And I'm Anna, and I'm smaller and I'm lighter." Anna replied. "Major wants you to come and meet Mr. David." She escorted him to the dining room.

Major Thornton said, "Little Jim Sykes, this is my son David." They shook hands. David was a little taller than his father and strongly resembled him.

"Little Jim will be working with the horses along with Chester. He came highly recommended by Ira, the blacksmith."

"I hope you'll like it here, Jim," said David.

The Major and David ate in the dining room, the help all ate in the kitchen at a long table with long benches on both sides. They ate mashed sweet potatoes and corn bread along with the chicken and dumplings. Jimmy had rarely taken a meal anywhere besides home and he carefully watched to see how the others conducted themselves, but he realized that his manners were no different than theirs and he began to feel at home.

Maj. Thornton and David wore white shirts with the cuffs rolled up and black trousers. They didn't wear ties. The climate was much too hot and humid to allow for that formality on a daily basis.

Chester was about forty years old and of average height and build. He wore boots and black trousers like the Thorntons with a blue denim shirt.

Brooks wore brown trousers and shoes and a white shirt with the sleeves rolled up.

Mattie, Chara, and Anna wore light cotton dresses with floral patterns with moccasins on their feet. The major had provided them with shoes which they begged him not to make them wear in the house. The moccasins were a compromise.

After supper Chester said, "Little Jim, are you coming down to the stable with me?"

"If that's ok with these folks." he replied.

"That's fine with us." said Brooks. "But don't be gone too

long, we need to show you around the house." It made Jimmy feel special that everybody was talking about him.

Little Jim and Chester made their way down to the stable. It was a fairly large building that covered a third of an acre. In the nearby pasture there were a dozen mares with six colts that were born that year. Jim had never seen that many tall and graceful animals at one time. He and Chester strolled down through the stable and looked at the colts that were born before that year.

"Now this one is Redbird," Chester announced, "Major loves this horse. He says he looks just like ol' Darley in the pictures of 'im." Redbird came over and showed his head over the stall door. "Redbird, this is Little Jim, you gonna be workin' with him. You gonna be knowin' him real well. What you think Jim?"

"He's beautiful, I never seen a horse like that. If the Major love him, I guess I do too."

There were other colts with names like Mockingbird, Meadowlark and Sugar Babe. There wasn't one that wasn't a fine horse.

When Jimmy returned to the house, the two housekeepers were ready to show him around. His bed was in a room with Mr. Brooks, which opened off of the kitchen. The outhouse was in the backyard and so was the pump. In a special room, that opened off of the kitchen, was a bathtub. Not just an old washtub, but a real bathtub. It sat on four feet, about five inches from the floor. When bedtime came, the boy couldn't fall asleep for hours- just thinking about everything in this house and on this land. It didn't seem real, this big farm that belonged to just two men, and it was all just to raise horses for racing. Finally he dropped off to sleep and dreamed about riding these handsome horses and letting them run as fast as they could.

Chapter 5

Pearl had sent Essie Mary to the druggist for some chamomile. She was wearing a simple white cotton shift which fit just a little tight. She had an old red scarf tied over her corn rowed hair. As she opened the door, the bell rang and Ben Tilton looked up and smiled at her. "Mama needs a nickel's worth of chamomile," she said.

Ben opened the jar and filled a small sack with the herb. "You're one of Miss Pearl's children aren't you," he asked.

"Yes sir, I'm Essie Mary White," she replied.

"Your brothers do some diving in the river in the summertime don't they?"

"Yes sir, they do. They find mussels, what are good eatin'. And they find some beads too. They shoot marbles with 'em mostly, but Mama save a few sometimes."

"Indeed. Well, tell your mother that I'd like to see them sometime. They can be worth some money. And if I buy any, I'll be glad to give the boys some glass marbles they can shoot."

"Mama will be glad to know that. She would be proud of the boys to be able to help her that way."

"Ask Miss Pearl to stop in sometime, I'd like to talk with her."

"Thank you Mr. Tilton, I'll tell her."

Ben couldn't help feeling that the children in the Yellow House had an advantage in life, if only because their mother was a forward thinking woman. He only wished they had more substance to their food and clothing. Maybe the pearls might bring them a little income to help in that respect.

Mitch and Matthew were outside the hotel sawing boards to the dimensions they needed to make the porch. Mitch had suggested that they could round off the corners to make the appearance of the structure more appealing. "But would the judge like the idea of that?" Matthew inquired.

"He might, or he might not," Mitch replied, "but he hired *me* to build the porch, so I think it should look like *I* built it."

Matthew chuckled, "Can't argue with you there, bucko, can't argue with you there."

Clothilda appeared at the hotel door with a pitcher of water and two glasses. "I thought maybe you boys would like a drink of water."

"You thought rightly ma'am," Matthew replied, we've got a sawdust thirst."

While she was filling the glasses she asked, "What is the nature of a 'sawdust thirst'?"

Matthew took a long drink and said, "'Tis not so much the nature but the degree of the thirst. You might call it a 'powerful' thirst. Thank you ma'am for the refreshing of our spirits."

"And my thanks as well." Mitch added.

"Tell me something gentlemen- if you can, I've heard that Gunner Jake is making a pair of boots for Jimmy Sykes. Maj. Thornton ordered them. Now why would the Major want the boy to wear boots?"

"Well now, I think I might know the answer to that question, Miss Clothilda," Mitch said, "But I have to ask you another question."

"What question is that?" She replied.

"Have you ever had a shod horse step on your bare foot? The boy will be working with the Major's horses, working around shod horses in your bare feet can be painful."

"Ahh... I never thought of that. Well, no, I've never had a horse step on my foot, but I think I might have some idea of what it would feel like."

Clothilda returned to the hotel kitchen and Mitch and Matthew returned to their carpentry.

Mitch said to Matthew, "I know you're happy with your accommodations at your campsite, but Reverend Davis has said that, if there comes a storm, you know the kind, with the wind and the lightning, that you are always welcome to come to the vicarage for shelter."

Matthew smiled, "Well that's very kind of him. One never knows what the weather will bring. I might accept his invitation if a heavy storm comes."

Judge Jacobs came by and stopped, watching the boys as they were nailing in boards to their porch frame. Matthew stood up straight; Mitch thought the big man needed a break and he stood up and laid down his hammer.

"What do you think, guvnor?" Matthew asked.

"It's 'yer honor' son," the Judge replied, "And you are both doing well."

"Beg your pardon, yer honor, I have a question."

"What question is that?"

"Mr. Tate, who often stays at the hotel, what's his

occupation?"

"Seth Tate is an independent trader. He acquires goods of all sorts from south of here as far as New Orleans. He brings molasses, coffee, flour, cloth, the nails you are using, brass fittings, lamp wicks- all sorts of things we use here. He's an important man in this community. You've got a curiosity, Mr. Patterson, it shows your intelligence."

"It was Mitchell's idea, as well, to ask the question, he must be intelligent too."

Judge Jacobs chuckled, "Oh, I've known that since I met him, I think the two of you are assets to the town. Why don't we go inside and ask Clothilda to make us some tea." The boys agreed and followed the judge into the hotel. Mitch had a feeling that the judge wanted to have a conservation but didn't want to have it on the street.

Clothilda was standing in the kitchen doorway as they entered the dining room. "Will you fetch us a pot of tea and three cups, please." Judge Jacobs requested. They gathered around the big table. "We spoke of curiosity," the judge began, "Now I have questions as well. About this ferry of yours, Mr. Patterson, it's to be horse powered I presume."

"That's right, sir, would you like a brief explanation of the design?"

"I would."

"I'll need only one horse to pull the boat, but I'll keep two horses in case of a problem. The horse would do all the pulling from this side of the river.
I'll have a pulley about ten feet high across the river, and another elevated pulley on this side. The rope will stretch from the boat up to the pulley on the far side, and across to the pulley on this side, and to the horse harness. That will be just for transporting the boat from this side to the other. The boat will drag a rope as it crosses to the other side, and that rope will be used to tow it back."

"That sounds simple enough, Matthew," the judge replied, "I suppose you've got the distances and angles worked out for optimum effect."

"Yes I do, I've seen other horse-drawn ferries in operation and it's just a matter of using the right proportions for this location."

Clothilda set the teapot on the table and poured them each a cup. Matthew and Judge Jacobs added molasses to theirs, Mitch drank his plain.

"Would there be any need for another person on the far bank?" the judge inquired.

"There might be," Matthew replied, "My friend Mitch Hendricks might fill that position if need be. Or maybe another local boy if Mitch is occupied in some other pursuit."

Matthew and Mitchell went back to their porch building and the judge returned to his residence.

Two hours later Mitch asked his friend, "Would you be interested in dropping in to the manse this evening?"

"The manse?"

"I believe you would call it the rectory. Brother Davis has some very good cider."

"Ah, the minister's dwelling. I like good cider. So after Miss Clothilda feeds us we'll repair to the manse?"

"Then 'tis a plan," Mitch concluded.

When they arrived at the minister's home that evening there was a small rotund gentleman sitting at the table. He rose and extended his hand to Matthew. "I'm Eli Cotter, you must be Mr. Patterson."

"That I am," Matthew replied.

Reverend Davis said, "Please be seated gentlemen." He set four cups on the table and filled them with cider from a stone jug. "Mr. Cotter is our official bell ringer. We have a splendid bell which is not large, but is loud and has wonderful tone. It rings for services and for other special occasions."

"Now Mr. Patterson, let me ask you a question," brother Davis continued, "Do you take much interest in politics?"

Matthew was enjoying his cider, and he was wondering just which way the conservation was heading. "Why, no father, I really don't. There doesn't seem to be much hope for the Irish to avoid being pushed about by the British, that's why I came here. I just want to earn an honest living and be treated fairly."

"I completely understand you, Matthew. That is what most of us want. I came here to escape the contemptuous infighting in Britain. I realize you're Roman Catholic, we were the church founded by John Wesley. Years ago we were all just 'Christians', now we're many different factions and we all resent and mistrust one another. Christ Jesus taught us to love our neighbors, He surely must weep over the way we've become."

"How did we get this way, Vicar?" Eli inquired.

"'Tis all about worldly concerns. Property, money, political influence. What saddens me is that there is now a party known as the Native Americans, that wants to restrict voting rights to exclude the Irish and German immigrants."

"But surely that goes against democracy," Mitch put in.

"Of course it does," brother Davis replied, "We just fought a war over people's freedom, now they want to make some people inferior."

"Didn't Mr. Jefferson belong to a group that accepted all religions?" Matthew asked.

"Yes, he did, and I think we should do the same.

More cider anyone?" Mitchell rose and filled everyone's glass.

"Here's what we can do. We four men, we'll meet here whenever we see fit. Don't talk about this with anyone. If anyone asks, we're just having Bible study, which, in a way, is what it is. If anyone hears about any religious bickering going on, we'll talk about it and see what we can do about it. Are you with me on this?" Everyone raised his glass.

"Well Vicar," Matthew began, "Mitch has suggested that I come to services at your church."

"You're welcome here at anytime. Why don't we use our first names? Harlan, Eli, Mitch and Matthew." They all raised their glasses again.

"Now I'm not saying I'll become a Methodist"
Matthew began.

"That's fine," Harlan replied, "I don't want you to, the Lord didn't mean us to be a lot of opposing sects. But it's better for us all not to even discuss the matter with our neighbors, for we don't know what foolish ideas they have going on in their minds."

Chapter 6

The first weekend that Little Jim came home he had a pocketful of nickels. He gave one to each of his siblings. He tried to give Pearl a dime, but she told him to keep it for himself. "You're earning wages now, you need to learn to save your money.
Besides, you wouldn't have anything left for yourself."

"Yes I do, Mama, he paid me seventy cents."

"He paid you for Saturday and Sunday too?" He nodded. "Lord what a blessing it is to work for a man like him. You make him proud of you, son."

"That's what I'm doin' Mama. He wants that big red colt to fly like the wind and that's what he gonna do."

Pearl hugged her son, "Lord take care of this boy, I can't do it no more."

Wendell and Tyndall told their brother all about the catfish they caught in the river. "Mr. Patterson help us pull him out," Wendell exclaimed. "It was so big it took all three of us to haul him to the bank," Tyndall added.

"What else has Mr. Patterson been doing?" Jimmy inquired.

"Him and Mr. Mitchell been building a big flat boat to go across the river." Wendell began, "Sometimes they work at the hotel, sometimes they work at the river."

Tyndall continued, "Mr. Patterson got a silver medal on his watch chain with a cloverleaf carved on it. He put up a big tent down on the riverbank, that's where he stays."

"He sure is a fine lookin' man." Ivory mused.

Pearl chuckled, "You just dreamin' girl, but I guess it's no harm in that. Well, little Jim, what do they do up at the Major's place?"

"Well, Mattie, she cooks and the food is real good.
Brooks is the butler, and I sleep in the room with him. I got my own bed. Anna Lee and Chara Kee, they wash all the clothes and all the beddin'. Chester is the hostler, I work with him. I help him take care of the horses."

"Have you been ridin' em?" Essie Mary asked.

"I been ridin' 'em some, just at a lope. Major don't want me really lettin' em run 'til I get my boots from Mr. Jake. He don't really want me up close to them shod horses either. I got my foot stepped on at Mr. Ira's place one time," Jimmy grimaced, "It hurts to think about it."

By Saturday afternoon there were a dozen wagons around the courthouse. The country folks were in town to trade for a few things they needed which they didn't produce on the farm. The townspeople could usually expect to find fresh eggs, butter, buttermilk, cheese, and fresh vegetables which the farming folk brought into town. In a corner of the courthouse square was a grass-free, level area where a group of children were playing marbles. Some only had homemade clay marbles, some had glass ones. Occasionally there would be pearls that had come from the river, but since the druggist had begun buying pearls and giving out glass marbles to replace them, pearls were rarely seen.

In marbles, as with many games, it was common to see black and white children playing together. Maybe they were too young to have their innocence taken away. Wendell and Tyndall had a game going with two white children; Johnny Curley and Becky Lay. Becky was considered by most to be a tomboy, but she was a formidable opponent at marbles as well as other games. Wendell had a large yellow marble which was his taw. Over the course of less than an hour he had won three marbles from John and one from Tyndall. Johnny, in his frustration over losing a third marble, flung Wendell's taw into the street, where it rolled under a wagon belonging to Herbert Turley, a local farmer. Wendell quickly dived under the wagon to retrieve his prized marble. Mr. Turley grabbed a whip, yelling "Get out from under there!" But when he tried to swing the whip, his hand was stopped. Matthew Patterson was standing behind him and had grabbed the tail of his whip. He cursed at Matthew, and then the handle of the whip was jerked from his hand. A few people laughed and Mr. Turley turned red with anger and embarrassment. By this time the sheriff, Robert Tisdale had walked up.

"That nigger was spooking my horses." Herbert barked.

"For God's sake, Turley, he's only a child. Simmer down and behave yourself. Give the man his whip back, Matthew. If he pulls it out again I'll take it away from him."

The dust settled and most went about their business. The sheriff leaned over to Matthew and asked him to drop by his office while he was in town.

An hour later Matthew showed up at the jail. Sheriff Tisdale asked him to sit down. "I just wanted to have a word with you," he began, "You didn't do anything wrong. These people here, the whites and the coloreds both, are mostly good people. There's a few idiots like Turley, but most of them, if you treat them with respect, you'll get along fine. Just act like this incident never happened, most of them will be your friends. I know you're going to be running a ferry and I'm glad for that. I think most of us are. If you run into any trouble in town, come see me. That's my job."

Pearl White had told her boys that when they were through with a game of marbles that the best thing they could do was to give back the marbles they had won to their original owners. Like it or not, there are some who are sore losers and it's best to avoid having people holding grudges.

Mitchell Hendricks was interested to know what Matthew and Sheriff Tisdale had talked about.

"Well I'm not sure I really understood what he was saying. He was mostly talking about respect, but I don't know if he was talking about the giving or the receiving of respect." Matthew said.

"Was it in regard to negroes and whites?"

"Yes, I believe so," Matthew replied.

"I think I can enlighten you about that subject," Mitch said, "It has to do with where the white folks came from. Some people once owned slaves. Or they've had colored folks work for them. These folks don't have a problem with talking to the colored folks. But then there are many whites that have had little or no contact with negroes and they resent them. And they also resent the white folks that deal with the colored race."

"That is an idea that is hard to get hold of," Matthew replied. "I don't see where that resentment comes from."

"Well, it's likely that those white folks feel inferior to the wealthy white folks and they feel a need to be superior in some way, to somebody."

"I think I see. So does that mean that I seem to them to belong to the upper class?" Matthew asked.

Mitchell commented, "I think it's quite possible that there are some who believe that you came from the land-owning gentry in the old country."

Matthew smiled, "I don't know whether to feel proud of their mistake or have pity on their ignorance."

Early on a Monday morning Jimmy came to the livery

stable. Ira had shod two horses for Maj. Thornton and Jimmy was going to assist Ira in bringing them back to Darley Hill. Ira was still in his underwear when he arrived. "Mornin' Little Jim, it must be daybreak. Saddle that mare for me, son, while I drink some coffee, this be much too early for decent folks to be stirrin'."

When Ira had drunk two cups of coffee they started off. Little Jim rode one of the horses bare back and Ira led the other with a long cotton rope. When they approached the cabin of Gunner Jake, the occupant appeared in the doorway. Ira called out, "Mornin' mister Jake, has you got something to tell us?"

"Yes, I do Mister Blacksmith. I got young Jimmy's boots ready. We won't put 'em on him right now, I'll bring 'em up later. Y'all just tell the major I'll be up directly and we'll try 'em on then."

Jimmy was grinning with excitement. The first time in his life he wouldn't be barefoot. He told Jake he would relay the message to his employer. "I can hardly wait," he said excitedly. As he followed Ira up the hill he looked back once or twice to see if Jake was coming. When he was sure that Jake was following he looked ahead and saw the arched gate of Darley Hill. He asked himself if this was really happening or if it was just a dream.

Practically the whole family was standing on the big front between the white columns. The two maids said, almost in unison, "Hey, little Jim." He felt a little flushed as Chester lifted him down from his mount. Then he took the lead rope from Ira's hand. He handed the lead rope to Chester, who led the two horses down towards the stable. By this time, Big Jim had descended the steps. He took Little Jim by the shoulders and lifted him and set him on the porch.

Ira said, "I done brought the horses back, but I ain't leavin' 'til I see that boy in them boots."

Jake finally arrived and dismounted- the new boots in his hand. He walked over and handed one boot to Jimmy. Chara quickly stepped over to his side. "Wait, Jimmy, you got to have stockin's," she said as she handed one to him. Everyone had a good vantage point as he donned the sock. Then he pointed his toes into the boot and pulled it up. It felt strange to have his foot so confined. Chara handed him the other sock and he slipped it on. Then he stood up on one booted foot and pointed his other toe into its boot. Soon he was standing with both feet in his new boots.

Major Thornton said, "Walk around, son. How do they feel?"

"I don't know how they suppose to feel."

Jake said, "Walk over this way Jimmy, let me feel your toes." Little Jim walked over to the edge of the porch where Jake was standing on the ground. The man pushed down with his fingers on the toe of one boot. "Do you have a little space around your toes?"

"Yes, sir I do."

"Rock from side to side; see if you have a little space on both sides." Jimmy did as he was instructed, and Jake declared the boots fit well enough. He bid goodbye to the household, then mounted up and rode away.

Big Jim was almost as excited as Little Jim. "Chester, let's saddle Redbird and we'll let the boy take him for a run." East of the house there was a large, oblong, area that was fenced with poles and planks. It was only about half the size of a real racetrack, but it was large enough for training purposes. "Let's saddle Dancer and, Chester, you ride him along with Little Jim on Redbird. Now don't mount up until we're inside the paddock."

When Chester and the boy reached the stable, they first led Dancer into the aisle and put the pad and saddle on his back. Then they led Redbird out. Chester fitted him with a bridle and had Little Jim hold the reins. Then Chester laid a saddle pad across his withers, and then the light racing saddle. Finally he tightened the girth- just snug enough so the saddle wouldn't slip back. As they were walking toward the paddock, Chester told Jimmy about what he needed to do. "Let him lope, but don't push him. Just let him stretch his legs good. Dancer and me will be beside you, just stay with us. We don't want to let him 'barn run' so be ready to hold him back comin' this direction."

Big Jim met them at the gate to the paddock. Chester held the reins while the major lifted the boy onto the big colt's back. They adjusted the stirrups so that Jimmy's knees were bent at a right angle. The major held him by the bridle until Chester had mounted. Big Jim let go of the bridle and let Redbird fall in next to Dancer. In seconds they were at a trot, then immediately into a lope. Going at a smooth clip, neither horse was straining. Big Jim guessed that they were back at their starting point in about sixty seconds. He made a mental note to measure the length of the oval fence. Watching his red colt devour the distance in an unhurried gait gave a lift to his spirits. He was getting closer to his moment of truth and feeling exhilarated. He let the riders circle the paddock five times, then signaled them to come in. When they dismounted, Maj. Thornton asked the boy how he felt.

"I feel like we could beat anybody, sir."

"Let's hope we can. How do the boots feel?"

"I gotta get used to 'em, but they feel all right."

"Well, I want you to wear them anytime you're around the horses. Can you do that?"

"Yes, sir, I will."

"Well, let's take the horses back down to the stable and feed them some corn. Chester, we need to get a bench for this boy to stand on so he can do any of the grooming that needs to be done."

When they got to the stable, Dancer was a little damp from the exercise, but Redbird hadn't broken a sweat. While the big red colt was eating his corn, Jimmy stood on an overturned bucket and used a brush to rub him down. Brushing was a way of establishing a relationship between a horse and a human, the same way feeding and watering does.

Maj. Thornton sat in a chair near Jimmy and Redbird. "How do the boots feel, son?"

"They feel all right, sir,"Little Jim answered, "just kinda...close."

"You'll get used to them,"said Big Jim,"they'll protect your feet. You need to think about keeping safe all the time. You know not to get stepped on, but try not to ever fall off. If you feel yourself start to slip, hold on tight to whatever you can. You can get hurt real easy by falling, especially when they're running- especially in a race. Will you do that?"

"Yes sir, I'll try."

Chapter 7

Matthew Patterson's tent was octagonal in shape. It was eight feet from one side to the other. The center pole was seven feet high. That was high enough that, when he was close to the center pole, he could pull his britches up while standing. A square tent, or even a hexagonal one, wouldn't stand in the wind as well. It would take a very large storm to generate strong enough wind to trouble his tent. One night in June there came a storm of that caliber. The morning had started off clear, but by mid-afternoon the clouds had started to gather, and when the sun was low in the sky, the wind had started to kick up. "There's a gale on it's way," he thought, "this might be the time to accept Brother Davis' offer of hospitality."

Over in the Yellow House, Ivory and Essie Mary, were closing the windows and fastening the shutters and the twins had come inside to escape the blowing dust. "Mama, Mr. Patterson's gonna be in for a bad night over in that tent," said Ivory, "reckon we could ask him to come to the house 'til it blows over?"

Pearl smiled, "You girls think a lot about that man, don't you. Well if it gets to rainin' hard, one of y'all can go over and see if he wants to come to the house."

"I'll go," Ivory said, "and it's gonna rain hard."

"Or I can go," Essie quickly added.

"All right, Ivory you go, and take that oilskin with you, and be careful."

By the time Ivory had the oilskin and started out the door, a burst of rain drummed on the roof. She was barefoot and wearing a light cotton dress that quickly became wet and clung to her body. Soon there was a lightning flash, and a thunderbolt close behind. She tried to set off in a line so as to avoid following the river, but she couldn't see her way, and she decided to follow the riverbank. She had trouble holding the oilskin in the wind and it was almost pulled from her hands a couple of times.

Finally she saw the tent and was able to reach it even though her feet kept slipping on the wet ground. She called out to Matthew, but there was no reply. There was no light to be seen from the tent. Finally she found the main flap and stepped inside. She called out to him several more times but it soon became apparent that he wasn't there. Sadly she walked back out into the storm and headed home. It was very dark by then and she had difficulty finding her way. When she got to the door, Pearl pulled her inside and told her to go sit by the stove.

"Mama, he was gone!" she cried.

"Well, I reckon he went to the church when he saw the storm comin', you tried to help, bless you."

Everyone who lived at Darley Hill was out by the small track, and Maj. Thornton had asked them to participate in a training exercise. "I want everyone to stand along the outside of the fence. Chara and Anna, will you both stand at the far end. Mattie, will you stand near this side. Brooks, will stand next to me near the gate. David, please stand on the other side of the gate. Some of you, put your hands on the top board and one foot on the bottom board.
We will all be looking into the interior of the track.
Will everyone pretend we have placed a bet on a horse and we're urging them on to win. Talk loudly and call out as if we are spectators at a race."

Chester and Little Jim , riding Sugarboy and Redbird, were at the gate. The major opened the gate and let them in, then closed it behind them.

The major announced, "On my command the horses will start circling the track and we will all be making noise. Now!"

The two horses broke into a canter, then gradually into a full gallop, circling the oval counterclockwise.
Little Jim noticed that Redbird tended to stay away from the people and he gently prodded him to stay close to the fence. This was precisely why Maj. Thornton was performing this exercise, so that the colt felt comfortable under real track conditions.

After they had completed three laps around the enclosure, Big Jim motioned them over to the gate.
He walked up to Little Jim on Redbird. "How does it feel, my boy?"

Jimmy replied, "He gettin' the hang of it. He'll get used to it in a little while."

"Good, good. Take him down and feed him some corn right away, just as soon as you get him unsaddled. We want to show him we like what he's doing." the major instructed.

Mitchell Hendricks was finishing up one afternoon when Judge Jacobs asked to have a word with him. "What can I do for you, sir?" Mitch replied.

"I'd like for you to take a message to Maj. Thornton, I'll add two bits to your pay. You can use my horse." said the judge.

"I'd be happy to, sir."

"Ask the major if it would be convenient for me to pay him a visit day after tomorrow."

"I'll take the message to him, sir." After Mitch put his tools away he strolled down to the livery stable to collect the judge's horse. Judge Jacobs' horse was a grey gelding named 'Cloudy'. Ira saddled and bridled him and Mitch set off for Darley Hill.

It was a sunny afternoon. Mitch gave the horse his head and he broke into a trot. In fifteen minutes he was at the bottom of the hill. Mitch was curious to know what the Thornton place looked like. He admired the wrought iron arch that said 'Darley Hill'. Mr. Brooks had seen him approaching from a quarter mile away, and was standing at the porch steps when he arrived.

"Mitchell Hendricks, I'm here to see Maj. Thornton." he said as he dismounted.

"Let me tie your horse and I'll take you to him." Brooks replied. The major was sitting on the couch in the living room.

"Ah, Mr. Hendricks isn't it?" Big Jim exclaimed.

"Yes sir," Mitchell replied, "I've brought a message from Judge Jacobs.

"Sit down, sir, thank you Mr. Brooks. What does the judge have to say?"

"He wants to know if it would be convenient for him to pay you a visit day after tomorrow."

"A visit, ah yes, as a matter of fact I was planning to have a going-away luncheon for my son David that day. Tell him he is welcome to dine with us if he would arrive before noon. Would you like a cup of tea?"

"A glass of water would be fine."

"Brooks, are you there?" The butler stepped into the doorway. "Would you bring Mr. Hendricks a glass of water."

"Right away, sir." Brooks replied.

"How is your friend Mr. Patterson doing?" the major asked.

"In general he is doing well. He is nearly finished with his flatboat. And it should be a sturdy vessel."

Brooks handed him the water. "Thanks," he said to Brooks, "Where is your son going, Major?"

"David plans to go into the shipping business. New Orleans and St. Louis are in this general area, but he's first going to try his luck in New Orleans."

"I wish him success in his undertakings. I've passed through St. Louis, and I've heard so much about New Orleans."

Mitch bid the major goodbye and rode back into town. It crossed his mind that Darley Hill seemed like such a lovely place to live, why would one want to go searching abroad for something better.

Maj. Thornton felt he had a decision to make. He had planned for his son's luncheon to be held in the kitchen with the help. By adding the judge to the party it became slightly larger than the kitchen table would seat. Besides, he didn't want to possibly offend Judge Jacobs' sense of dignity to sit with the colored folks. He would need to mull over the idea a little while.

Two days later, Mattie was up early fixing breakfast. She boiled enough rice that, after breakfast there would be enough to serve at dinner.
Chara was making biscuits and Anna was stringing and snapping green beans. Company was coming. It was only one person, Judge Jacobs, but she wanted everything to look nice and for the food to be the best she would serve. And she was anxious to meet the judge.

Judge Issac Jacobs arrived on horseback at eleven o'clock. Jimmy took his horse to the stable while the judge ascended the porch steps. Brooks met him at the door and ushered him in. It was common practice for a horse to be left tied to a post outside a building, but Maj. Thornton believed that if you treated a horse better, he would serve you better. If a visitor was staying longer than a few minutes, the animal would be led to the stable where there was water and feed; the bridle was removed and the saddle girth loosened.

"Judge Jacobs, I'm so glad you could come," Big Jim exclaimed.

"Happy to be here, Major. You have a lovely home."

"Thank you, sir. Allow me to introduce my son, David."
They all shook hands with one another. The servants were
lined up in the hall. "This my butler, Mr. Brooks," the major
continued, "my kitchen manager, Miss Mattie, my house
maids, Chara Kee and Anna Lee, my chief groom, Chester,
and my first jockey, Little Jim."

"Happy to meet all of you," Judge Jacobs said. They all
nodded their approval.

"Well, you all go about your duties, the Judge and Mr.
David and I will sit in the drawing room and wait for
dinner. Will you have a glass of sherry, your honor?"

"Why, I believe I will, thank you."

While he was pouring the sherry, the major began,
"This is a special occasion, your honor, by special I mean not
just a celebration. You see, David is going off to New
Orleans to enter the shipping business, and it may be a very
long time before he returns. My wife died some years ago
and David is my only close relative. My staff have seen
David grow up here and this celebration is as much for them
as for us." The judge smiled and nodded. The major
continued, "Now the plan was for David and myself to sit at
the table in the kitchen rather than in the dining room. If you
prefer to sit in the dining room I will accompany you, but
David would like to sit in the kitchen with the help."

Judge Jacobs looked up and chuckled, "Why Major, I
would be happy to sit in the kitchen. I get the feeling that
you respect these folks, and that's a good thing. Might I ask
if we could have a word with Chester and Little Jim before
dinner?"

"Of course we can," Big Jim replied, "Brooks, would you
ask Chester and Little Jim to join us."

Mr. Brooks stuck his head in the kitchen, "Jimmy, Chester,
Major wants to see you." Jimmy looked surprised. "Don't
worry, boy, you ain't in trouble," Chester kidded him. They
entered the sitting room and Big Jim asked them to sit down.
The judge looked at Little Jim, "You're one of Miss Pearl's
children, aren't you?" he asked.

"Yes sir, I'm the second oldest." the boy replied.

"Are you really, I thought the two girls were older."

"No sir, Essie Mary twelve, I'm thirteen."

"His small stature makes him a good choice for a jockey,"
Big Jim pointed out. "Chester tells me that he's a first-rate
horse handler."

"He was helpin' Ira with the horses for a long time before he came here," Chester added, "He probably done took care of Judge Jacobs' horse many times."

"The blacksmith has taken good care of our horses for a good many years now, if it weren't so,
we would have a hard time finding another. I imagine he will be looking to replace this young man." the judge opined.

Jimmy spoke up, "My brothers could learn to do that. They both ten, that's how old I was when I start helpin' Ira."

Judge Jacobs said, "Chester, do you think Jimmy's brothers would be good help for Ira?"

"Yes, sir, I do. The main thing is they love horses, and they can learn from Ira."

Judge Jacobs continued, "David, I understand you plan to go to New Orleans. You might find it helpful to speak with Seth Tate. He travels back and forth to New Orleans quite often."

David said, "Yes, sir, I have talked with Mr. Tate several times. He gave me the addresses of several people in the New Orleans area that he has done business with. He has been very helpful to me."

"Dinner will be ready soon," Big Jim told them, "We'll be having smoked ham, green snap beans, rice and gravy, and biscuits, and I think Mattie has baked apple pies. I hope everyone has an appetite."

"If you never had Mattie's apple pie," Chester said "it's the best you ever had."

It wasn't long before Mr. Brooks was at the doorway saying, "Dinner is served."

The kitchen table was not quite large enough to seat nine people, so a small tea table had been brought in to stand at the end of the kitchen table.
All the servants, plus David Thornton, sat at the kitchen table, while Maj. Thornton and Judge Jacobs sat at the tea table. Chara and Anna served the two older men first, and then David. Then the dishes were passed around to everyone else. No one spoke for several minutes, then David said, "I'll miss you folks... all of you."

Mattie dabbed at her eyes with her napkin, "We'll miss you too," there was a long pause, then she continued, "you always been a good boy, I just hope you be careful, we care about you."

"You know I'll be careful, and I won't be gone forever, I'll be back to visit."

"Will you be riding down on horseback?" the judge inquired.

"No sir, Chester and I will be driving down with Mockingbird. He's an older brother of Redbird and a fine horse. That's why I feel sure that Redbird will do well."

The judge went on, "Racing is popular in the state of Kentucky, Major, but did you know that there are plans being made to begin horse racing in Hot Springs?"

"I've heard of that," Big Jim replied, "frankly I would welcome racing into this part of the country.
Racing in Hot Springs would include Kentucky bred horses along with animals from other areas. My own horses came from Kentucky as well. If racing became successful here in Arkansas it would enable me to earn income with my horses."

Little Jim couldn't help thinking how wonderful it would be if racing came to this place and he would be part of it, along with the major and his beautiful horses.

It wasn't long before Mattie asked if everyone was through eating and if they wanted pie. There was titter of laughter, as if anyone didn't want pie. Chara and Anna cleared the dinner plates first, then began serving the pie. The judge and the major got theirs first, then they started serving the rest at the big table. Jimmy wondered if the rest of the staff noticed that the two white men didn't start eating their pie until everyone was served. David said, "Mattie, I'll miss this pie almost as much as I miss you."

Judge Jacobs stayed and talked until the afternoon shadows had started to lean. Jimmy led Cloudy from the stable. "Wait a moment Judge while I tighten his girth," said Chester.

"You mean you've made him at home while he was here?" the judge inquired.

Chester replied, "Sho' have. We took his bridle off, and gave him hay and water."

"Oh my, Major, you treated me and my horse as well as you could. I've enjoyed this thoroughly. My compliments to every one of you fine folks." Chester helped him onto his horse and he headed back to town. He couldn't help thinking that Jim Thornton knew some things about horses and people that many people would never know.

Chapter 8

The West Creek Baptist Church was a quarter mile south of the town square. It was a small, white, frame building without any distinguishing characteristics. The minister, James King and his wife Victoria, lived in two rooms in the rear of the church. Across the road was the home of Doctor Amos Biggs and his wife Helen. Wednesday night was Bible study for the Baptists and they were meeting this week at the doctor's house. Pastor King and his wife were there, along with Scotty and Elaine Shoal, and Herbert and Norlene Turley.

"Matthew, chapter three," Brother King began, "Jesus begins his teaching in parables. He tells of the sower who goes out to sow his seed. Now what is Jesus talking about here?"

The doctor answered, "I believe He's saying that he's the sower and the seed is his word."

"Does everyone agree with that?" the pastor asked.

Elaine said, "I agree, and he's letting them know they have to listen well because not everyone does."

"Of course they don't," Herb Turley put in, "Them niggers over in their church ain't got no idea what that's all about."

"Now you don't know that, Herb, they're Christian just like we are."Norlene replied. "What do you think Brother King?"

"Well the colored folks have the Abyssinian Baptist Church and we have our Baptist Church. When Paul went out to preach to the Gentiles, that includes every race besides the Jews. So Jesus is for all of us, not just white people."

Mrs. Biggs asked, "But Paul taught the Hebrews too, didn't he? So God must want to save the Jews as well."

"That's true," Scotty said, "but what about Catholics, like that Irishman. Didn't they all get off the true path?"

Elaine said, "Scotty, there's not a Catholic Church within a hundred miles of here, besides, his name's Matthew, just like in the Bible."

"That Irishman's a menace to the townspeople. You just mark my words." Mr. Turley yelped.

Dr. Biggs said, "Now, now, Herb, he just kept you from making a fool out of yourself. You need to learn how to get along with your neighbors."

"Ok, now what did Jesus mean about the seed that fell by the wayside," the pastor continued, "and got trampled underfoot?"

"Ah, well," Scotty droned, "the Lord's word just, sort of, gets ignored by some folks, kinda like they didn't really hear it, so it doesn't do them any good."

"Mr. Shoal," the pastor commented, "that's as good of an interpretation as I've ever heard. But now, does that mean we should quit bothering to spread the word, because nobody listens?"

"No, we just keep on spreading the word, because every now and then somebody does listen, and that's what makes it all worthwhile." Scotty replied.

David Thornton left Darley Hill in the buckboard with Mockingbird in harness and Chester driving. The whole household was out on the front porch to see him off. Mattie gave him an embrace and he shook hands with all the men. His father said, "Good luck, son, and write when you get a chance."
David nodded his head, Chester clicked his tongue and they rode off towards town. It was early morning and the square was deserted. When they reached the ferry landing they stopped to confer with Matthew Patterson.

"Good morning gentlemen, you must want to cross the river," Matthew said to them.

"Yes we do," David Thornton replied, "I'm on my way to New Orleans to seek my fortune."

"Well, you'll be the first to use the ferry who's bound for the Mississippi river. I, myself, followed the Ouachita river to here from where it forks off of the Mississippi. We'll take the horse across first, then we'll take the carriage across. We might be able to squeeze them together, but we're in no hurry and I'll only charge you fifteen pence, er cents, for the crossing."

Chester unhitched Mockingbird from the buckboard and led him onto the flatboat. The gelding was visibly nervous but Chester spoke to him reassuringly and he didn't try to bolt. Matthew had the collar on the white mare and he tied on the rope. He clucked to her and she began pulling the boat out into the river. After a few minutes the boat was on the eastern bank and Chester led the horse off of the boat.

Matthew switched ropes and the mare towed the boat back across the stream. Together, Matthew and David lifted the carriage wheels over the gun-whale and onto the boat. David paid Matthew the fare and shook his hand before climbing on with the buckboard and ferrying the stream.

Chester and David took turns driving as they made their way east toward the Mississippi river. Mr. Tate had told him that his own route to New

Orleans was by way of the Pine Bluff to reach the Arkansas river. But that meant traveling for a good sixty or seventy miles north when they were already south of where the Arkansas joined the Mississippi. They figured to travel east by the best roads they could until they reached the floodplain and then try to approach the town of Eunice on the Mississippi. David would buy passage down to New Orleans and then Chester would return to West Creek. David had a pencil and paper to try and make note of the twists and turns along the way. If they found a good route, Chester would have the notes for future reference. They knew that someday there would be a good road to follow, as the Mississippi river would be the main north-south route in their part of the world. St. Louis would surely grow and New Orleans would become a cosmopolitan city. So there had to be a major jumping-off point between the two. Arkansas Post had been that place, where the Arkansas joined the Mississippi, until the shifting of the river had forced it further west. As they pushed on along an eastern wagon track a fragrant odor began to fill the air. "What's that sweet smell?" David inquired.

"That's honeysuckle," Chester replied, "It's them little white and yellow flowers, they grow all over in the woods."

"Oh my, "David commented, "to think something that sweet-smelling would just be growing wild out in the woods."

"And the bees and hummin' birds like it too."

"I'll bet they do. I know it's possible to follow a bee back to it's hive."

"They say there's folks that got tame bees what make honey." Chester mused.

"They do indeed," David answered, "Maybe someday we'll have folks around here that keep bees."

"And all these purty little yellow and white flowers will get turned into honey. They sweet already, you know." Chester said.

"Are they really?" David commented. He reached down from the wagon seat and broke off a sprig of the flowers.

"Pull off the flower and suck on the back end."

David did this and exclaimed, "They are sweet, who would have thought... there's another resource this land has to offer. It's just here for the taking."

"I hate to see you go, Mister David," Chester said.

"I know, you all do, but I want to take a try at the shipping business." David replied.

"It ain't just that, it just seems like things bound to change with you leaving." Chester paused for a moment. "You see, some of us got to work for white folks to get by, and you and the major, nobody treat us as good you all do."

"I think I understand what you mean, Chester, but aren't there any other white people you can expect to treat you right?"

"Well, maybe a few, the doctor, the judge, Mr. Mitchell— Little Jim says Mr. Patterson is a good man."

"Well, you know what I would do, if there are any colored folks that you know that get mistreated by white folks, make sure no colored folks will work for them. That might get them to change just a little bit."

"Well, that does seem like a good idea. But you know, there's some white folks that don't want nothing to do with us. Won't hire us, won't even talk to us. That's the ones we really worry about."

"Ah yes, I think I know the kind you mean. I think a lot of them came from the Scotch-English border. They don't want to talk to anybody that's not like them. They are a worrisome group of people. Now if you know about somebody being hurt by those people, let the major know. He's friends with the judge, and the sheriff, and other important people."

"But what about other colored folks besides us that don't work for the major?"

"Well, I'd ask for his help anyway. He'll do what he can."

"Well, thank you, sir, that helps. But you know, I think it's going to be a long, long time before we can trust most white folks."

"Yes I know, Chester, it will be a long time, but the best we can do is for the good folks to stick together and don't give up hope."

By the time the sun had begun to reach the western horizon they reached a crossroad, and an increase in wagon tracks suggested they were approaching a community.

"There's a settlement down here called Hamburg," David announced, "it might be a good place to spend the night."

"That's fine with me," Chester replied.

After they had gone about five miles they could see activity ahead, it was a young but thriving community and there was a sign that said, 'Hotel Carlton.' They stopped in front of the building and David climbed down from the wagon seat. Chester waited while David went inside. The clerk stood up as he approached the desk.

"I need a room for myself, and do you have a place for my colored help to sleep?" David inquired.

"Yes sir, we have a vacancy for you and we have a bed in a room on the ground floor for your help.
Your room will be fifty cents and your nigger's bed will be twenty-five cents."

David signed the register: 'David Thornton and employee Chester Burns'. He wanted the man to understand that Chester was a trusted, paid helper.

"Your room is upstairs, first door on the left. Your...helper's room is the first door to my right."

David had Chester help him carry the trunk upstairs, then they went to look for a livery stable.
They found one a block down the street. A black man named Charles was tending the stable. They left the carriage and the horse in his care with instructions to feed some corn to the horse. Then they returned to the hotel.

"Let's go look at your accommodations," David said to Chester.

"My what?" asked Chester.

"Ah, your bed." The room was dimly lit and David looked around for a lamp. When he found one he struck a match and lit it. There were four beds in the room.

"I'll be fine here, sir," Chester allowed.

"Well, feel of the beds and pick the most comfortable one."

Chester tested the beds with one hand. This one is fine, I'll sleep on it."

"Well, leave your bag on it and we'll go find some food to eat. I think this hotel has a kitchen."

They found the dining room and didn't sit at a table, but stood by the kitchen door. A black waiter approached. "May

I serve you sir?" he asked.

"I'd like to speak to the cook." David replied.

The waiter nodded. He stepped into the kitchen and said, "Rosetta, a man wants to speak to you."

She soon appeared. She was a middle-aged woman, fairly tall and thin. David said, "Ma'am, do you have a table in the kitchen where my helper and I might have something to eat?"

"Yes, sir, but you don't have to eat in the kitchen."

"Thank you, but I hate to eat alone. What do you have prepared?" David inquired.

"I have ham and sweet 'taters, rice and gravy, field peas and mustard greens." Rosetta replied. "I'll fix you all plates and you just sit at the big table."

The food was good and there was plenty of it. David couldn't help feeling a little apprehensive. He was far enough on his way that he couldn't turn back. He had to make it in the shipping business- failure was not an option.

They retired to the bunk room and sat and talked for several hours. Chester commented on Little Jim and his horsemanship. "He's a brave and smart little boy. I think the major made a good choice when he hired that boy."

"I just hope he doesn't get hurt," David replied, "the ground is a long way down for him."

"It's a long way down because he's a tall horse, it's the same long way down for anybody. Many a man has fell from a horse goin' at a dead run and didn't have nothin' bad happen." Chester said.

"Hmm, I never thought of it that way," David said.

"Besides that, Jimmy is as good a rider as I've ever seen. He's rode tall horses at a full gallop ridin' bare back and now he's got stirrups, so I don't think he's in any danger," Chester explained.

David said, "You know, that makes it seem like I've been worrying too much about it. Thanks for telling me about that."

As David Thornton climbed the stairs to his room he couldn't help thinking that if it was up to him, Chester could sleep on another bed in the same room. They were traveling together anyway. Suppose one of them had an ailment of some kind in the night. The other person could go for help. It was a change that would have to come about some day; who knows when or how. It was a long time before he got to sleep; there was a lot on his mind.

When he looked around and saw daylight, he rose and dressed before going downstairs. Chester was already up and was standing near the desk.

"Good morning Mr. David, Rosetta has hot rice and coffee on the table and she's fixin' to have eggs and bacon."

"Just what I need to get me going, Chester, did you get a good rest?"

"Oh, yes, I went down and got Mockin'bird into harness already."

"Oh my," David replied, "You must be in a hurry to get back home."

"Oh, yes, but I'm thinkin' about seein' Eunice, and the big river too. I ain't never seen it before."

The bottom land of the Mississippi river was mostly forest of gigantic hardwoods. Oak, pecan, sweet-gum, cedar, willow, and cypress. Trunks so large that three men with outstretched arms could barely match the circumference. It was hard to imagine the vast amount of lumber they could be turned into, or the number of buildings that could be constructed from that amount of lumber. With the huge amount of fish and game found there, the native people must have lived a life of abundance before the land saw the coming of European people. David couldn't help wondering that if the land became cotton plantation, would the owners be able to make a profit without their free labor. From what he knew of the local community of West Creek, the former slaves seemed inclined to stay and work for what wages they could get rather than venture off into unknown territory.

Chapter 9

They reached Eunice in the middle of the afternoon. The town was buzzing with activity. As they approached the town square the could see the top of a steamboat on the river. "I believe I'll go talk to somebody about that steamboat," David said, "Chester why don't you find the livery stable and I'll meet you later in front of the hotel."

"Yes sir, I will," Chester replied.

When he got to the dock, a boatman told him that the captain and the purser of the vessel, the 'Emily Marie', were in the hotel bar room. As he entered the room, David saw two men in nautical attire, sitting at a table. He approached the table and introduced himself. "Good evening gentlemen, are you connected with the Emily Marie?"

"We are," the older man replied, "I am the captain, Blake Elliot, and this is my purser, Robert LeJeune. Won't you sit down."

"Thank you, I will," David replied, "I'm David Thornton and I'm headed for New Orleans."

"We are bound for New Orleans, would you care to travel with us?" said Captain Elliot."

"I believe I would, when do you depart?"

"We'll leave in the morning," the captain replied, "Would you like a beverage, sir?"

"Some tea would be nice," David answered.

"Would you like it iced? We just happen to have brought some ice down river with us and there is a block in the kitchen."

David looked amused. "Why, an iced tea would be very nice, excuse me a moment." David went to the hotel entrance to see if Chester was there. He was, and David asked him to come inside.

Capt. Elliot had risen and stepped to the bar to order the tea. He looked back at David who was puzzling over where to have Chester sit. The captain picked up a chair and set it in back of David's chair and a little to the side. He motioned Chester to sit there.

"This is Chester Burns, my hostler, gentlemen. This is Capt. Elliot and Mr. LeJeune."

"Let me guess, Mr. Thornton, you're from the North." the

captain pronounced. "A chair a little back is accepted etiquette for the help in the South."

"Thanks, I'll remember that. My father and I are from Kentucky. He was a cavalry officer in the Union Army and we moved to Arkansas after the war. I'm on my way to New Orleans to go into the shipping business. I borrowed Chester to drive me to Eunice."

"Interesting, I'm from Illinois, myself. Tell me, what does your father do in Arkansas?"

"He raises thoroughbreds. Chester is an excellent horse handler, invaluable to the family. There may be racing going on in Arkansas in the future. But I have always wanted to have a go at the shipping business."

A waiter approached with, not one, but two glasses of iced tea. Blake thanked him and handed him a quarter. Chester grinned as David handed him his glass. "Thank you so much sir."

"Thank Capt. Elliot, he ordered it." Chester thanked him.

"Where'd this ice come from," Chester asked.

Mr. LeJeune replied, "Originally from Canada. In the larger cities in the Northeast they store it packed in sawdust. I believe it is a high-profit business. Now I don't want to dissuade you from traveling to New Orleans, but you should look into the way that railroads are expanding nearly everywhere."

"Yes, I've noticed there is one being built right here in this town." David agreed, "River traffic has to connect with land traffic somehow."

"And the railroad is the most efficient form of land shipping," Capt. Elliot put in.

"That's certainly something to keep in mind." David commented, "Now what time will we be sailing in the morning?"

The captain said, "We'll knock on your door, Mr. Thornton, when we rise tomorrow."

"I haven't registered in the hotel yet for myself and Chester." David answered.

The captain replied, "Why don't you go and register and then we'll order supper. With your permission, Chester could bunk in the crew sleeping quarters on the Emily Marie."

David asked Chester, "Would you like to do that?"

"Oh, yes sir, that would be fine."

They found a small table and set it a few feet away as a dining table for Chester. The black waiter that brought Chester his plate remarked with a smile, "They treatin' you like a high yaller now."

Chester smiled back, "Long as they treat me like a grown man, that's all I care."

Chester was given a bunk below decks on the riverboat. It felt a little strange, he felt sort of isolated, even though there were other folks sleeping in other bunks on the boat. There was a sort of rocking of the whole vessel which was not unpleasant, but he could understand why the captain and the purser had stayed in the hotel- probably to have a break from constant movement of the bed.

At dawn he hurried back to the hotel so he could enjoy breakfast with David and the two boatmen.
Again he sat at a small table a few feet away from the other men, but he felt like a partner rather than a lackey.

Once breakfast was over, Chester and David made a last farewell. The trio of men bound for New Orleans made their way to the Emily Marie while Chester proceeded to the livery stable.

Chapter 10

Chester paid the man the money he was owed and led Mockingbird out to the buckboard and backed him between the shafts. By the time the harness was all attached it had begun to sprinkle. By the time he had driven to the outskirts of town it was a steady drizzle. He knew from experience that the country could easily deliver a torrential downpour and he was glad to be moving away from the river bottom. The sky was gray and heavy in every direction. The temperature was about sixty degrees so he didn't feel cold, but he worried that the rain might get heavier and the temperature might drop.

After traveling about a mile, he noticed a large oak just a little way off the trail. He decided to seek this relative shelter and perhaps avoid getting chilly and wet. He guided the horse close to the tree and got off the buckboard. He realized that the horse and rig would not fit under the tree, the branches were too low to the ground, but then he noticed that the horse could get under the tree if he approached the trunk of the tree straight on. He unhitched Mockingbird and led him under the branches of the tree. The gelding seemed to understand they were getting out of the rain and he proceeded to lie down. Chester sat down under this massive tree and thought about the idea that he would have been better prepared for the weather if he had an oil-skin. He made a mental note to mention it to Maj. Thornton when he got back to Darley Hill.

In a couple of hours the rain let up. The sky remained overcast, but there was only the dripping of the rain from the tree, so he decided to push on.

Late in the afternoon they were back in Hamburg. He remembered the man named Charles at the livery stable and he headed there.

"Mister Chester. On your way back home?"

"Oh yeah, ran into some rain on the way, got a little wet," Chester replied, "think I'll spend the night and go home in the morning."

"Well, we'll find a place for the horse. If you want you could sleep in the hay loft, or did the white folks give you money to stay at the hotel?"

"Well, the major give me money for the trip, but I can

always save a little for myself."

Charles chuckled, "I know about that, tell you what, I'm fixin' to go eat supper with Miss Rosetta real soon, why don't we go over together?"

"That suits me fine," Chester replied.

Chester drove Mockingbird into the stable, they unhitched the buckboard and led the horse into a stall. When they had given him some hay Charles said, "Let's go see what Rosetta's got for us to eat."

Chester and Charles went around to the back of the hotel. There was sign above a doorway which read, 'colored'. It was the back door to the kitchen.

When they knocked,, Rosetta opened the door. "Well, your name is...Chester, right?" She said.

Chester replied, "That's me. Me and Charles are mighty hungry, what you got cookin'?"

"I got fresh buttermilk, cornbread I baked this morning, smokey ham left from dinner and...*sweet tater pie.*"

"Oh lord," Charles exclaimed, "we come to the right place. Woman, bless yo' heart."

"Well, y'all sit down at the table and I'll bring you a plate." After serving the two men, Rosetta sat down at the table with a glass of buttermilk. "I never knew anybody what lives over west of here. What's it like over in Union County?" she asked Chester.

"Well, my boss told me they made Union County for a place for folks from up north to come to, but they ain't many of them. They's just some white folks who ain't got much, but the homestead law made it so they could move there. And colored folks could use that homestead law. Our preacher is tryin' to find out how we could do that too."

Charles said, "But yo' boss is from up north?"

"Yeah, he was in the calv'ry. Just him an' one or two others is from up north. But I'm lucky to be workin' for him. He treat everybody right. But most the colored folks- and they ain't many of us- was already livin' there 'til we got set free."

"So what do yo' boss do?" Rosetta asked, "Is he a farmer?"

"No, he raisin' race horses. He got a big house and a lot of land an' I'm number-one hosteler. That means I take care of the horses. An' he treats them horses just like he treats his help. Them horses are never scared, they know we won't never hurt them. Little Jim Sykes is his jockey. He ain't but fourteen years old and he don't weigh but eighty pounds, but he's as good a rider as I've ever seen. Now look here, how much this supper cost?"

Rosetta said, "Well now, I would've been throwin' food out. So let's just say y'all don't owe me nothin'."

Charles said, "I ain't gone charge you nothin' for sleepin' in the hayloft, so all you got to pay me for is what that horse eatin'."

Chester said, "I got this money that Maj. Thornton paid me for this trip. I'm goin' home tomorrow and I got left two dollars and a quarter. What do you say we split this money three ways, so we all have some?"

"Fine with me," Rosetta grinned.

"All right with me too," Charles added, "but what is two dollars and a quarter split three ways?"

"Well two dollars is eight quarters," Rosetta began, "so one more makes nine quarters. You make three piles, that's three quarters in each pile, so we each get seventy-five cents, am I right?"

"I believe you're right," Chester said as he pulled the money out of his pocket. He had a silver dollar, two half-dollars, and a quarter.

Charles said, "Give Rosetta a half-dollar and a quarter. I got a cash box over in the stable, we'll change that dollar over there."

"Well Miss Rosetta, it's been fine meetin' with you, if you ever come to Union County, come see me at Darley Hill."

"I will do that Mr. Burns, have a good trip home."

The two men walked back to the livery stable.

When Chester left the next morning he had a feeling of accomplishment. He had driven David Thornton to Eunice on the Mississippi, he had spent the night on the riverboat that would carry David to New Orleans. He had made some new acquaintances along the way. He had saved the major the expense of his lodging in Eunice and also in Hamburg. He had had a nice visit with Charles and Rosetta in Hamburg, and he had rewarded Charles and Rosetta for their hospitality. Now he was returning to Union County with a half-dollar and a quarter in his pocket.

Chapter 11

Maj. Thornton invited horse owners from all over Union County and the surrounding area to drop in and have dinner with him and his staff. Not many of these horses were "hot-blooded" but there were a few that were. This gave him the opportunity to let them run their horses against his. It was good training for Redbird, and it gave his neighbors an idea of the caliber of horses he kept. Some might become interested in having their mares bred by his stallion. Just talking about or reading about horses had a certain amount of appeal, but watching a truly fine animal in action would make a far better impression.

Little Jim woke on a Wednesday morning and could hear a discussion going on in the kitchen, He quickly dressed in his shirt and trousers and walked barefoot to the kitchen. Chester and Brooks were already at the table.

"Morning L'il Jim," Chester said, "You gonna have a big day."

"It ain't my birthday." Jimmy replied.

"No, you get to ride a race today." said Chester. "The Beasley family got a stallion they been breedin' for a few years. They done challenge the Major to race against Redbird."

Little Jim felt butterflies in his stomach. He didn't know what to say. Chara was setting bowls of rice and milk on the table. He took his bowl and started dripping syrup from the pitcher on it. "Today? Where this gonna be?"

"Up the River Road to the Sumacs, 'round the big oak tree and back- 'bout two miles."

Jim was having a hard time eating his rice. "You all ain't just jokin' with me?"

Brooks chuckled, "No, it's true. Reckon you can do it? I know you can."

"I can do it. Oh lawd, yes!"

"That's my boy," Chester said with a smile.

Breakfast was over soon. Chester was enjoying a second cup of coffee and he told Jimmy to go on down and call the horses into the stable. Jimmy poured a ration of dried corn into the manger in each stall.

There were five horses in the small pasture and they were all waiting outside the gate when Jimmy let them in. Each one knew which was his or her stall and they all eagerly started eating. Little Jim went around and shut the stall doors. There were another fourteen brood mares in a larger pasture beyond a row of cedar trees. They would potentially produce colts that might become racehorses.

When Chester arrived he began to fill Jimmy in on the agenda for the day. There would be perhaps a dozen or so people arriving around the noon hour.

"For lords sake boy, where's your boots? You go on up to the house an' get 'em on."

Little Jim made a mad dash for the house and was back in five minutes. "I'm ready now Chester," he exclaimed, "What can I do now?"

"Just relax, now. Catch your breath, sit down there on that bench, then get the brush and go in there and lead Redbird out here and give him a good brushing down; don't forget to talk to him."

Jimmy did as Chester told him. He stood up on the bench and brushed across the horse's back. "Redbird, just relax boy, we gon' run today. They got some ol' black stallion gon' try to keep up wit' you. Don't you worry, we know how to run. He don't. How you feel? You look like you feel good. I feel good too." Chester was stifling a laugh.

Maj. Thornton soon arrived. "How's Little Jim this morning?"

"I'm fine, sir."

"If you want to, put a saddle on him and ride back and forth to the front gate a couple of times. I want to get him used to having a few people around. Get him to stay relaxed. We're all going to stay relaxed, aren't we Chester?"

"If you say so, we gon' try."

The Beasley family had a big farm which lay to the south of Maj. Thornton's place. They raised livestock of all kinds. Their closest neighbors were Will and Letty Henson, a black family who had an eighty acre homestead south of the Beasleys. Jake Beasley's black stud horse was the sire of many riding and carriage horses in the area. Jake Beasley and his wife Sarah arrived at Darley Hill right about the noon hour, driving a light carriage and leading the black horse behind. Chester and Little Jim unhitched the carriage horse and tethered him with a long rope. The black horse was also tethered with a long rope and Jimmy put a bucket of water where both horses could reach it. The Beasleys ate dinner with Maj. Thornton in the dining room.

As soon as Jimmy and Chester were through eating they walked down to the stable to get ready for the race. Somehow Redbird seemed more alert than usual. He seemed restless and pawed at the ground a few times. Chester said to Jimmy, "Just stay behind him until the black levels off, then give him his head, all right?" Jimmy nodded. They tightened his saddle girth and Jimmy mounted and let him circle around to keep him calm.

They soon had Beasley's black bridled and saddled. Jake Beasley was not a large man, but he weighed about a hundred and sixty pounds. The major offered to add weight to Redbird to compensate for the difference, but Beasley declined.

The group casually walked down through the main gate and onto the river road. Maj. Thornton held Redbird by the bit and Chester held Beasley's horse. The major told Chester to release the black first and then he'd release Redbird.

The black horse accelerated nicely. In three seconds the major released his big red colt. In about twenty yards he caught up with the other horse. Little Jim gently held him back in an easy canter. They remained in that position until they reached the oak tree. As they circled it, the big colt was grunting and trying to stretch his neck. After an eighth of a mile Jimmy relaxed the reins and let him stretch out into a full run. He seemed to gobble up the distance. The black was beginning to tire, and Redbird stretched out his lead until, nearing the finish, he was eight lengths in the lead. Little Jim gently reined him in and circled back to where the people were standing. Redbird huffed and nodded his head. It seemed as though he understood what had been asked of him and he had prevailed.

"Do you plan to stand him at stud?" Mr. Beasley asked to major.

"Not just yet," Big Jim replied, "I'm going to take him to Hot Springs for a few days and let him run, and see how he does. Then we can think about breeding him."

"What fee would you be asking then?"

"I think maybe five dollars to begin with, and see how things go." Big Jim replied.

Jake Beasley nodded his head, "I charge two dollars for mine, and I didn't have much in the way of competition. You've got a fine horse there Major. Thanks for your hospitality."

"It's been a pleasure," the major replied.

Chapter 12

A black farmer named Will Henson lived about three miles
south and a mile west of West Creek. He had a wife named
Lettie and a daughter named Ida.
It was a homestead of eighty acres. He had one cow, one
horse, and a flock of chickens. Just north of his farm was the
three hundred twenty acre farm of Jake Beasley. He had two
sons, James and Jacob. He had cattle, horses, and hogs, as
well as a few head of Merino sheep.

One day, just after sundown, Ida Henson ventured
into Beasley's sheep pasture in search of sheep pills. Many of
the poor folk in that area of the country, who usually
avoided doctors, relied on folk remedies to treat their
maladies. There were roots, leaves, and berries which were
known to have healing properties. Sheep pills, the droppings
of domestic sheep, were used to prepare a tea which was
effective against several diseases, particularly measles.
Trying not to draw attention to herself, Ida was looking for
pills which were not too fresh, but not too dry. She had
picked up a handful and placed them in her apron pocket.
She was headed home when she was spotted by James
Beasley. James and Jacob had been squirrel hunting a little
distance away. They decided to investigate this act of
trespassing on their father's farm. Ida didn't notice their
presence and they circled around and apprehended her as
she was stepping over the sheep fence. She let out cry as she
fell to the ground and they each grabbed an arm.

"Please let me go," she pleaded, "I ain't done nothin', just
let me go home."

"What were you doin'?" Jacob snapped, "you were stealin',
weren't you."

"No sir, I was just gettin' sheep pills."

"You're trespassing. We're takin' you to talk to our Daddy."

They couldn't be persuaded to release her and they were
soon at the Beasley abode.

Will Henson became worried when his daughter didn't
return. He told Lettie he was going out to look for her. When
he saw no sign of her in the sheep pasture, he ventured on to
the Beasley home to ask if they had seen her. Jake met him at
the door in apparent hostility. "Yes, I've seen your daughter,
my boys caught her trespassing on my farm, and she's going

to stay right here until the sheriff gets here. My son is on his way there now."

"Please, just let me take her home, she won't come here no more, I swear." Will entreated.

"I can't have people coming on my place and taking whatever they want, I've got to put a stop to this," Jake snapped.

"Daddy," Ida wailed, "Tell 'em I ain't done nothin' to them."

"It's gonna be alright, Baby, don't worry."

Will sat down on a stump at the front of the house. It seemed to him like some white people went out of their way to cause trouble for black people.

In about a half hour Sheriff Tisdale came riding up. Jake came out of the house, still in a snit, "Arrest this man or arrest his daughter, we caught them trying to steal from us."

"All right, Beasley, just simmer down, I'll handle this. Now this girl, what's her name, Henson?"

"Ida, sir."

"All right, where was Ida?" Tisdale asked.

"She was in my pasture, stealing." Jake barked.

"Well, it's late," the sheriff sighed, "Henson, bring your daughter, we'll go into town."

"I'm filing charges," Jake thundered.

"I told you I'll handle this, Beasley, you can say whatever you want to the judge. Just come into town tomorrow. " C'mon Henson, let's go. We'll talk about this on the way."

The sheriff lifted the girl into the saddle and he and Will walked on down the road. After they had gone about a quarter mile Sheriff Tisdale asked, "Now was Ida in his pasture?"

Ida replied, "Yes, sir, I just went in there to get some sheep pills. I ain't done nothin' else."

Robert Tisdale frowned, "Sheep pills? What kind of pills?"

"Sheep droppin's," Will explained, "when folks is sick, you make tea with the sheep pills."

"Oh my lord," the sheriff groaned, "That's what you were stealing from Beasley?..... I'll tell you what, I'll take you folks home. Have you got a horse Henson?"

"Yes, sir."

"All right, you all come into town tomorrow afternoon, we'll get Beasley in here and we'll talk to the judge. I can't believe they got me out here after dark for somebody stealing sheep droppings."

The sheriff led the horse and Will walked along as they made their way back to the Henson farm. There was a moon out so it wasn't hard to follow the road, but dark enough that if any of the Beasleys looked out they would not be noticed. As they approached the Henson house Lettie came running out. She hadn't known until right then what was going on.

"Is my baby all right?" she cried.

"She's fine, Mama, them Beasleys was just causin' trouble, Sheriff just bringin' us home."

"Oh, thank you, Sheriff, I was so worried."

"It's all right, Lettie," Will told her, "We got to go into town tomorrow an' explain to the judge what it's all about."

Robert Tisdale lifted the teenager out of the saddle and Lettie hugged her tight. "You folks get some sleep and tomorrow come to my office and we'll go over to the courtroom. And Ida, don't go onto Beasley's place anymore."

"Oh, lord no, I won't go near that place, I swear."

The sheriff chuckled as he mounted his horse, and waved.

"Goodnight Sheriff, and thank you," Will called after him.

By ten o'clock the next morning the word had spread around town that a little 'colored gal' was caught stealing a pocketful of sheep manure. "Reckon they'll lock her up fer thirty days?" was the often heard remark.

There were an unusually large number of people in town for a Wednesday. Mitchell Hendricks allowed to Rev. Davis that he intended to be there, "If not in the courtroom, outside a window." Most of the people intended to make it look as though they just happened to be there, for no particular reason. The courthouse was a simple log and board, one room building. Inside were a table which served as a bench, and a dozen or so chairs.

Will and Ida were in the sheriff's office by one o'clock. Sheriff Tisdale asked Ida to stand by the window and look for Judge Jacobs to come out of his house. It was nearly two o'clock when he finally emerged and walked across the street and unlocked the courtroom. The sheriff, followed by Will and his daughter, made their way there. By two-fifteen Mr. Beasley and James and Jacob had arrived.

Mitch found a seat inside and most of the chairs were soon occupied. Ivory White was standing outside, close by an open window.

"The first order of business," Judge Jacobs began, "is the question of the Henson girl, being present on the Beasley estate, sometime yesterday. Mr. Beasley, is that correct?"

"Yes your honor, she was pilfering on my land when my boys caught her." Beasley asserted.

"Now when you say 'pilfering', what exactly do you mean by that, was she taking something of yours?"

"Yes your honor, she was," Beasley replied.

"Well what was it, Mr. Beasley?"

"Ah...fertilizer,"your honor." A noticeable titter went through the room.

"Could you be more specific, sir."

"Well, ask her, she knows what she was taking."

The titter in the room became a chuckle. The judge tapped his gavel. "Order in the court. Ida Henson, could you stand up please."

"Yes sir," Ida managed.

"Were you taking something from the Beasley farm?"

"Yes sir, sheep pills. See, when folks get sick, you makes some tea with sheep pills so they get better."

Sheriff Tisdale rose and whispered something to the judge. "Ah, you mean sheep droppings?"

"Yes, sir. I didn't think they'd mind, they got lots and they ain't usin' 'em." The people were trying not to laugh but it was difficult.

"All right, Mr. Beasley," What would you say is the approximate value of these, uh, sheep pills?"

"Well, I don't know, they're using them for medicinal purposes."

Mitchell rose to his feet, "May I say something your honor?"

"Very well, Mr. Hendricks, what do you have to say?" the judge replied.

"Your honor, if it would be any help I'd be happy to take up a collection and go to the livery stable. I'm sure Ira would sell us a tow sack full of horse manure to compensate Mr. Beasley for his missing sheep droppings."

The courtroom broke out into loud guffaws. Judge Jacobs was pounding his gavel on the table but he was laughing as well.

When the laughter finally died down, the Judge began, "Folks, I see a simple solution for this problem. Now there are several farms in this area that have sheep. Nearly everyone in the area comes to the livery stable from time to time. If everyone who owns sheep would bring a few, uh, pills to the livery stable, Ira would have a supply on hand to share with those of us who, uh, need them. Would all of you find that acceptable?" Everyone in the room was nodding and murmuring their assent.

"Now Mr. Beasley, do you claim to need to be compensated for your loss?"

"No, your honor."

"Will Henson, will you please ask your children to refrain from trespassing on Mr. Beasley's estate."

"Yes your honor, I will."

"Thank you, court is dismissed."

When Mitch stepped outside he saw Ivory talking to a couple of the village girls whose families she had worked for. When she saw him she smiled and said, "Afternoon, Mr. Hendricks, I heard what you said in there, that was the funniest thing I ever heard in my life."

Mitch said, "Well I think that sometimes a good laugh is what it takes to bring folks down to earth when they get all riled up. So it's really true that some folks make that tea for a sick person?"

"Oh yeah, folks been usin' that for a long time, just like they use chicory and willow bark an' all them things. Now I ain't sayin' that it always helps, it's just, you know, it ain't gon' do no harm."

Chapter 13

Boise Curley's farm was about a quarter mile north of the livery stable. He and his wife Lonnie had two sons, Boise Jr. and Johnny. Boise Jr. had the nickname Bobo. A number of farmers in the area had taken an interest in a planting experiment Boise was carrying out. He had twenty acres planted in oats. The land was too wet to raise wheat, so he was trying oats. Oats were good for horses and people. That was supposedly why the English had good horses and the Scottish had strong men. But oats needed a cool climate, so the strategy was to plant oats in the fall and hope that they would reach maturity in the early summer before the weather became too hot.

Boise had gone out to see if his newly planted oats were sprouting. Johnny, who was six years old, came along because anything his father was doing, he took a keen interest in. Bobo, who was four, tagged along because anything his brother was doing, he took a keen interest in. His mother Lonnie didn't realize he had left the house- neither did Boise or Johnny. He was fifty feet behind his father and sibling and rapidly losing ground because they were walking faster than he was able to. He was barefoot and wearing high-water pants, and his cotton shirt was sleeveless. The ground was a little muddy and his toes were sinking into the mud, which made his plodding gait just a little slower. He was not a child that whined a lot, and his cries, "Johnny and Daddy" were barely audible. He fell on his stomach, picked himself up, then slipped and fell again. He lay still there for a few minutes, thinking that, surely, his mother or father would soon find him.

He wasn't sure whether to keep following his father and brother or to return to the house. He decided in favor of the house, but he wasn't sure in which direction it was. He turned completely around and all he saw were bushes, and trees. No house, no oat field, no family. He couldn't decide what to do, so he decided to just keep walking in the direction that seemed like the way to the house.
His legs were getting scratched and he was getting thirsty.

The sun was getting close to the horizon and he realized that the direction of the sun must be west.
But west wasn't the direction he should go. He told himself

that he needed to go some direction that wasn't west. He kept plodding on. Then, up ahead, he saw water- he must be heading toward the river. His mother had always told him to stay away from the Ouachita river. It was too deep and swift to wade in. But at least he was somewhere close to town, because it was right next to the river. Besides, he was thirsty. He looked around for something to dip water with. He couldn't see anything that would work. He decided to creep slowly toward the stream and lie down on his stomach so that only his head would be over the water. He did this, and soon he was sipping the water. After taking a good drink, he retreated from the edge of the river.

It occurred to him that if he was up higher, maybe he could see people or buildings, or something to give him a direction in which to go. He looked around to find a tree he could climb. All the trees he could see didn't have branches low enough for him to reach. Then he saw a pine tree which rose out of the ground at an angle, then went several feet parallel to the ground before rising vertically. He could see that the branches would be within his reach. He climbed onto the trunk and began inching his way up. The first few feet were easy. He found that he could use his hands to pull and then push with his feet, and he got still higher until he could reach out his right hand and grab onto a branch, and then grab another branch with his left hand. This wasn't so hard. The branches were close enough together that he was able to climb higher and higher. He figured he might as well keep on climbing since the higher he got the better he would be able to see. After he had climbed about fifteen branches, he stopped and looked around. In one direction he could see across to the other side of the river, and a long way up and down the river. In every other direction all he could see was more trees. He couldn't see his parents' house or any fields. Then he looked down. It was then he realized he didn't know how to climb down from the tree. Even if he were to walk along the river bank he would have to get out of the tree before he could do that. He felt very tired, and he closed his eyes to take a little nap.

Boise and Lonnie walked back and forth through the woods expecting to find Bobo somewhere close by. They told Johnny to stay close to the house in case Bobo found his way back. After fifteen minutes they split up, with Lonnie looking toward the west and Boise looking east. After a good part of an hour had passed they decided to ask their neighbors to help.

Boise walked to the livery stable. He told Ira he was looking for Bobo, who had wandered off. Wendell and Tyndall were there and they volunteered to help. "Just tell us where you saw him last, Mister Curley, we'll help you find him," Tyndall said.

"Just walk on down past my house, he's in the woods somewhere." The twins trotted off in that direction.

When Mitch Hendricks and Rev. Davis got the word they headed over towards Curley's farm. Mr. Johnson from the general store was there, as well as his daughter Becky. The woods were dark, even when the sun was high, and as it got later into the afternoon it became even darker. Eventually half a dozen people were searching through the woods.

Bobo woke to the sound of someone calling his name. He looked down but he couldn't see anyone.
He called out, "I'm here," but his soft voice didn't carry very far, and he was about forty feet off the ground. The sun was dropping below the horizon and Boise and Lonnie sadly told their friends it was too dark to continue and they needed to wait until morning to begin searching again.

The Sykes twins told Pearl that they had been out looking for Bobo Curley. "I know," she said, "lot of folks was out looking for that boy; you all eat your supper and get some sleep, you can start lookin' in the morning."

While the boys were eating Wendell had an idea.
"Now s'pose he went over by the river 'cause he could see futher away."

"Yeah," said Tyndall, "s'pose he just keep walkin' along the river but he gone a long way. Let's look over there tomorrow." By eight o'clock they were in bed.

The twins heard a rooster crowing at five AM. No one else was up so they poured themselves some buttermilk and found some cold biscuits to eat. When the sun was above the horizon they set out to look for Bobo. As they had planned, they went to the river bank. They went to the ferry and started walking north from there. They took turns calling out "BOBO."

Tyndall said, "Let's call, then count to ten before we call again."

"Ok," Wendell agreed, "BOBO.....BOBO...you hear somethin'?"

Bobo heard his name and called out, "I'm here."

"I hear somethin'," Tyndall said, "Where's it comin' from?"

Wendell pointed up, "Up there." They both looked up and searched the trees. "Bobo, you up there?"

"Yeah, me." Bobo responded.

"There he is," Tyndall cried, "Bobo, what you doin' up there, come on down."

"I can't, I'm scared."

"I'll go get Mr. Patterson, you stay here," Wendell said, before running off toward the ferry landing.
Matthew and Wendell were back in minutes.

"He scared to come down." Tyndall explained.

"All right," Matthew said, "One of you boys climb up there, I'll get a rope."

By the time Matthew returned, Tyndall was half way up to Bobo's perch. "Here Tyndall, I'll toss you the end of this rope," said Matthew as he tied a knot in the end of the rope. "When you get up to where Bobo is, run the rope over a branch above him and tie the end around his chest."

It took Tyndall only a few minutes until he was up where Bobo hung on for dear life. There was a branch right above Bobo's head. Tyndall swung the end over the branch and pulled up a few feet of rope. "Hold yo' arms up Bobo," he coaxed.

"I can't," was Bobo's reply.

"Then raise one arm." Bobo raised one arm and Tyndall slid the rope around Bobo and slipped it under his arm pit. He tied it around Bobo's chest and said, "He tied on Mr. Patterson."

Matthew called, "All right Bobo, start backing down, I've got you." Bobo carefully put both hands on the tree trunk and started easing down. Matthew felt his weight and cautiously played out the rope as Bobo slowly descended from the tree. Tyndall decided to wait until Bobo was all the way down before he started climbing down.

Matthew played out the rope a few inches at a time until Bobo's feet touched the ground. Matthew told Tyndall to wait while he untied Bobo. Wendell took the boy by the hand, "Yo' momma gonna be glad to see you, boy."

Matthew pulled the rope back up to where Tyndall was sitting. Tyndall tied the rope around his chest, just like he'd done with Bobo, and Matthew lowered him down. When Tyndall was on the ground Matthew told the twins to lead him into town. "Hold his hand and walk up the trail to Ira's place, then turn and go up in back of the stable."

With Wendell holding Bobo's left hand and Tyndall on the right, they marched triumphantly up the trail into town. "Miss Curley, we found Bobo! Mr. Curley we found Bobo!" By the time they'd reached the livery stable there were people making their way in their direction.

The Curleys soon arrived and Lonnie was squeezing her boy and saying, "Thank you Lord! Thank you Lord!"

The butcher, Mr. Greenwald, said, "Thank those little colored boys, they found him."

The twins were a little embarrassed when Lonnie started squeezing them and saying, "Oh thank you, thank you, God bless you boys for finding my baby."

Wendell and Tyndall made their way back to the Yellow House. Pearl said, "I'm so proud of you boys. How did you find him?"

"He was up in a tree, Mama." Wendell explained.

Tyndall added, "Didn't nobody look up in the trees but us. And we heard him hollering, "Here I be, here I be."

"Mr. Patterson helped us." said Wendell.

"What did Mr. Patterson do?" Pearl wanted to know.

Wendell went on, "He brought a long rope, and Tyndall put it over a branch and tied it on Bobo and Mr. Patterson lower him to the ground."

"I see," Pearl commented, "that man is all ready to help whenever anybody needs him. But why didn't he bring Bobo in to town?"

"I don't know, Mama, he just said, 'you boys hold his hands and lead him into town', that's what he said."

"I think I see," Pearl said, "he wanted folks to know you all care about children and be ready to help if anybody need us."

By the afternoon, Mr. Johnson brought them a twenty-five pound sack of flower; Mr. Greenwald brought a side of bacon, and Mr. Curley brought them a chicken. For the next few days 'finding Bobo' was the topic of conversation and the oft heard remark was, "Thank God he was all right."

Chapter 14

David Thornton was taking advantage of the early spring weather by taking a walk along the Mississippi levee in mid-afternoon. The air was humid, but it always was in New Orleans. It was a clear day and from the top of the levee he could see for three miles up and down the river and north through the city an equal distance. He had been in the port for over a month, working for the McDermott company, helping keep their accounts.

As he strolled west along the levee he caught occasional snippets of conversation from people fishing in the borrow pits at the base of the levee. The words 'Dieu' and 'que poissons' could be heard.

A few lovebirds could be seen walking hand in hand or lying in the shade of a cottonwood tree. In the distance he heard a woman's scream. He stood and listened for a moment. A few seconds later he heard the sound of hoof beats. Soon a riderless horse ran out of the woods, ascending the levee and coming in his direction. Instinctively he raised his hands to shoulder height and started calling, "Whoa, whoa, whoa." He let his hands drop, then raised them and dropped them again.

The horse broke stride into a trot, then to a walk..

Continuing to say "whoa, whoa," David walked up to meet him and put a hand up to pat him on the neck. He reached up and caught hold of the reins. The horse's nostrils flared; he was breathing very hard and was apparently scared. He was a tall, well-built, black gelding and wore a French riding saddle and a silver-decorated bridle. His breathing began to slow and David continued patting him on the side of the neck. A black-haired girl was approaching from the same direction as the gelding and she was sobbing as she walked. She was a stunningly beautiful young woman, and David wished he could take her in his arms and comfort her as he was doing with her mount.

"Merci, monsieur, merci," she said through her sobs. David handed her a handkerchief which she used to wipe her eyes and cheeks. She could see David was struggling to understand her and she quickly switched to English.

"I fell off! He saw..."

"A snake?"

"Yes a big snake!"

"He was just scared" David said, "He's young and scared. He'll be okay now."

"Oh, thank you sir, how did you make him stop?"

"Oh, they depend on us, you know. We feed them and care for them, don't we?"

"Yes, I suppose we do."

"He ran up the levee because it's open and, well, free of snakes. They trust us, what else could they do? I'm David Thornton."

"You're a kind man, David Thornton, I'm Camilla Bourgeois. Would you like to meet my family?"

"Yes, I would," said David.

Camilla smiled, "Why don't you come to dinner tomorrow. We live at the very end of Carondolet Street. Do you know where that is?"

"Yes, I'll be there," David replied. He helped her to get mounted and she smiled as she rode away.

Chapter 15

Little Jim had been working for the major for one year and Redbird was a three-year-old. In February Maj. Thornton got a letter from the track steward in Hot Springs. Racing would begin at the track on March twenty-first. He told the staff about it at breakfast the next morning. "Are we going Major?" were the first words out of Little Jim's mouth.

"I've already sent in the entry," the major replied.

All the boy could do was smile. He'd literally dreamed about racing the red colt, but he'd always woken up before the finish. Now he felt his heart pounding in his chest. All around him the others were jabbering, "Well I declare...My, my...Ain't that somethin'."

The major chuckled, "Take it easy, it's more than a month and we'll be ready, won't we."

"Yes, sir, we will," was all Jimmy could say before he went back to eating his rice.

After breakfast Maj. Thornton asked Chester and little Jim to sit down with him in the dining room and address the coming adventure. They could have talked in privacy at the stable, but Big Jim wasn't worried about being overheard- in fact he expected it. "One thing I'd like to do," he began, "is to ask Ira to make some shoes for Redbird suitable for racing."

"That's a new one on me," Chester declared.

"Well you see," the major explained, "horse shoes start out at about half an inch thick, then they get worn down to where they are a quarter inch thick in places and to nearly nothing elsewhere. That's when they get re shod. For racing you want a shoe that is a quarter inch thick to begin with."

"But a new shoe with hard corners?" Jimmy inquired.

"Exactly," said the major. "Now I'm going to ride into town and talk to Ira and see how we go about getting the right kind of horseshoes for Redbird. Also, we need to be thinking about anything to prepare ourselves for the coming day of reckoning."

"Day of reckoning," Chester said, "I guess that's what it is."

Chester saddled Mockingbird and Big Jim rode into town. February was early spring in south Arkansas and it was a very pleasant day. Along the way he started thinking about silk. The racing stables in Kentucky each had a certain color of silk that represented them. He thought of the red and white stripes of the U.S. Flag. He hadn't heard of any stable using those colors, and in any case, no stable in Arkansas did.

"Good morning, Ira," the major said as he approached the livery stable.

Ira stood up from his anvil and came toward Mockingbird. "What can I do for you this morning?"

"Give this horse an armful of hay, I need to talk to you about horseshoes."

"What kind of horseshoes you talkin' about?" Ira asked as he led Mockingbird into a stall.

"Well, I'm thinking about shoes for my racehorse, frankly, what kind of stock do you use to make horseshoes?"

"I use three eighth inch iron rod, for ridin' horses, half inch for workhorses."

"I want a shoe that is, roughly, a quarter inch thick, and the normal width with no heel. By my calculations that would require between a quarter and five sixteenths rod. Do you have any rod that size?"

"What does that come out to?" Ira asked.

The major paused for a second, "Five thirty seconds."

Ira said nothing for several seconds. "I might have, let me look." He walked into the barn. He didn't return for several minutes. When he did return he was holding a rather thin metal rod in his hand. "It ain't iron," he said,"it's bronze, and it's five thirty seconds."

Major Thornton smiled, "Ira, you're a natural-born wonder."

"Well, I'm a blacksmith, sir, I got to have my stock. A while back the judge's wife wanted some bronze curtain rods, an' they had to be just the right size. I reckon it'll make fine horse shoes."

"Here's what we'll do. You go ahead and make the the shoes. In a couple of weeks I'll bring him into town and you can put them on. My goodness this worked out well. I'm going to stop in and see the judge, can you take care of Mockingbird until I return?"

"Yes sir... oh Major,"

"Yes?"

"Would I be able to place a bet on Redbird?"

"You know, you're about the tenth person who's asked me that. Sure, Ira, when we get ready to go to Hot Springs I'll take your money then."

Big Jim walked over to the judge's place and rang the bell. Mrs. Finchley answered the door. "Come in Major, won't you sit down, I'll get the judge."

Judge Jacobs said, "Good afternoon, Jim, what brings you to town?"

"Well, I just came in to talk to the blacksmith about making a set of horseshoes for racing purposes, and I must add that it's lucky that Mrs. Jacobs ordered bronze curtain rods. Ira had some left over stock that will be perfect for horseshoes for my red colt."

The Judge chuckled, "Well I'll be. I'll have to tell Mildred about that. How is your boy David getting along?"

"He's temporarily employed as a bookkeeper for an engineering company and he's met a beautiful French girl. That's about all I've heard. "the major replied.

"He's a smart young man, I'm sure he'll prosper. Tell me, who all is going to Hot Springs for the races?"

"Just Little Jim and myself, Isaac. That way Chester can take care of the livestock, and Brooks can manage the household, I'm sure the boy and I can shift for ourselves while we're away," Jim replied.

"Would you like some tea, Jim?" the judge asked.

"Ah, no, I should be getting back, I've got plans to carry out."

When Big Jim returned he took Chester and Little Jim aside. "Ira is making some special shoes for Redbird. They'll be bronze and a quarter inch thick."

"Why bronze?" Chester inquired.

"Ira just happened to have some bronze rod of the right size. Actually bronze has been used for horseshoes for hundreds of years. We only started using iron when metallurgy gave us a hardened iron which could be wrought rather than cast." Maj. Thornton explained.

"What does that mean?" Jimmy asked.

Big Jim chuckled, "You see, cast iron, that we use to make stoves and skillets, is breakable. If you hit it with a hammer it would break. But when you add other things to it like lampblack, or other metal, it gets stronger. That's what our horseshoes are made from. Bronze is a mixture of iron and copper and it's very strong. Not quite as strong as wrought iron, but it won't wear down in the time between now and the race. Ira didn't have any iron the right size but he just happened to have bronze. Little Jim and I will ride into town tomorrow on Mockingbird and Redbird and the shoeing will commence."

Again, Jimmy had trouble getting to sleep. The idea of Redbird getting bronze horseshoes seemed real special, like when he first put on his boots made by Gunner Jake.

They left right after breakfast. Big Jim asked the boy to ride Mockingbird, he wanted to ride his big red colt- he weighed a hundred and seventy pounds so he wasn't a heavy load for a three-year-old. It gave a little bit of a thrill to feel the strength in the gait of his young thoroughbred. They trotted most of the way, but they went into a canter for about half a mile as they were approaching town. Then they pulled up and were at a walk as they approached the hotel. A few heads turned as they continued on to the livery stable. The two 'Jims' both had a feeling that most of the townspeople were captivated by the idea that a locally born and bred horse was about to challenge the the 'sport of kings'. "Well look who all's come to see me this mornin'," Ira announced as they stopped in front of the big oak tree.

"Good morning Ira," Big Jim said with a smile.

Ira had the forge hot. He had fashioned shoes from the bronze bar. Jimmy and the major dismounted. Mockingbird was led into a box stall and his bridle removed. The boy gave him an armful of hay to keep him occupied. Ira removed Redbird's bridle and replaced it with a simple halter so Jimmy could hold his head while the blacksmith worked.

"Hoo, boy," Ira said as he lifted one of the red horse's front hooves. He held one of the shoes against the horse's foot. "Got this shoe just a little wide, we'll fix that." Ira set the foot back on the ground and went to the anvil. He laid the shoe in the forge and then picked up the hoof rasp and went back and picked up the horse's foot. With a few quick passes of the rasp he evened off the edges and flat surface of the hoof. Little Jim kept Redbird's attention by talking to him and with slight pressure on the halter. Ira picked up the shoe from the forge with a pair of tongs. Holding the shoe on the horn of the anvil, he beat on the side of the shoe to make it narrower, then he quenched it in the water bucket. Holding the shoe against the front hoof he was satisfied the fit was good. Holding half a dozen hoof nails in his teeth, he took the hammer and drove the nails through the holes in the thin shoe and clinched them. Then he took a pair of nippers and clipped off the nail ends. He let go of the foot and Redbird put his weight on it.

"How does that feel, Redbird?" Ira asked. The red colt grunted.

The major laughed, "I guess that means it feels good."

Ira proceeded to work on the other front foot. This time he did the necessary rasping before comparing the shoe to the hoof. When he had the shoe nailed in place and released the foot, he heaved a sigh and straightened up. "You all know, when he wins that race and y'all come back from Hot Spring with that trophy, this town's gonna be mighty proud."

"Well, Ira, it may not happen that way, we can only try," Big Jim said, "but we appreciate your confidence."

"That's all right," the big man said, "he was born here, you trained him, Little Jim rode him, I shod him, we just gonna be proud no matter what."

"We're going to try our best, aren't we Little Jim?" the major said."

"Yes, indeed, we will." Jimmy replied.

Ira commenced with the shoeing of the sorrel colt's hind feet. When he was finished, he said, "Now Majuh', if you interested, I got two more shoes I made from the rest of the bronze."

"Oh, very good Ira, I'll take them along when we go to Hot Springs. They might very well come in handy. Now how much do I owe for your services?"

"It comes to two dollars and a quarter for the six shoes and the shoein'. What do you say you give me a dollar and a quarter and bet the other dollar for me on the race." the blacksmith allowed.

"I better write down all these bets so I don't forget. Do you want to bet him to win, place, or show?" Maj. Thornton asked.

"Do I what?" asked Ira.

"Place and show are for second or third." Big Jim explained.

"I'll go for the win, then." Ira replied.

"All right then, Jimmy, go get Mockingbird, I don't want to be late for dinner."

Little Jim rode Redbird on their way back to Darley Hill. He could feel a subtle difference in the horse's gait- like he was stepping on freshly plowed soil and didn't want his feet to get dirty. He was smiling and the major said, "All right son, let me in on it."

"He's steppin' different, sir, like he's thinkin' 'I got me some new shoes', you know?"

"Sort of like you were when you got your new boots?" Big Jim suggested.

"Yeah, I guess so, sir." Jimmy replied.

Early in the afternoon Wendell and Tyndall came by to talk to Ira. "What you boys been up to, today?"

"We was thinkin' about divin' for mussels but the water still to cold," Wendell related.

"But we was walkin' a long ways down the river when we look across an' there's a big ol' mess of vines growin' over across the river." Tyndall commented.

Ira raised his eyebrows, "'Bout how far down?"

"Far?" Tyndall said, "Oh, 'bout four or five times as far as it is across the river. We was thinkin' about getting Mr. Patterson to take us across so we could see if they's possum grapes or if they's muskydines."

"That ain't too far," Ira mused, "Tell you what, don't tell nobody about this. Mr. Patterson, he knows I make wine, but don't say nothin' to him. Let's wait about a week til them berries start to make an' we'll go across an' look, all right?"

The boys agreed.

Chapter 16

David Thornton was up early. He had an appointment to see a Mr. Hartmann whose office was a short way from the docks. He had been staying in a boarding house close to the old quarter. The landlady was a matronly creole woman, very prim and proper. The food was good and the bed linens were changed twice a week. After he had eaten breakfast and drunk two cups of extremely thick, black coffee, he walked over to Mr. Hartmann's office. The man had not yet arrived so David took a seat on a wrought iron bench on the sidewalk outside. Since it was early, the air temperature was still pleasant. He looked up and a stylishly dressed man was standing in front of him. His hair and beard were streaked with gray and he carried a gold-tipped cane. "David Thornton, I presume?" he asked.

David nodded. "I am Eli Hartmann. Won't you step into my office, sir." He unlocked the door and held it open for David. "I've been in New York on business. I believe you are acquainted with Mr. Seth Tate."

"I am," David replied.

"Tell me, I have forgotten, where is West Creek Arkansas?"

"Not far north of the Louisiana border and about one hundred miles west of the Mississippi River." David answered.

"Tell me about your background." Mr. Hartmann said.

"My father, Maj. James Thornton, and I are from Kentucky. He served in the Union Cavalry in the war. At the age of nineteen I entered Duke University and spent three years there before joining him in Arkansas. My mother died when I was a small child."was David's reply.

"Have you been in New Orleans long." Mr. Hartmann asked.

"About a month. I've been helping to keep the accounts at the McDermott Company, but that, of course, isn't shipping." David replied.

"Ah, you're more interested in shipping."Mr. Hartmann said, and David nodded. Well let me describe the outlook in the shipping business as it now stands. Since the nineteenth century began, the steam engine has given us industry as we've never had before. As you're probably aware, steamboats can carry us up the Mississippi and Ohio all the way to Pennsylvania. Then, of course, there is the railroad, which will, in time, connect towns all across the continent. The Western United States has been connected to the East by way of sailing ships. Now that the war is behind us those trails that led to the West will become railroads. Do you catch my meaning, Mr. Thornton?"

"Oh, yes I do, sir, but I have a certain urge to see travel across the oceans." David answered.

"Well, of course you do, many a young man does. Let me make you an offer, I can use someone of your education in my operation. I do a fair amount of trading with cities in the Northeast, and at the present time, the quickest way is up the Atlantic coast by steamboat. You can help me with my accounts, and when I have another trading mission across the Gulf and the Atlantic, you can make the trip with me. But, in the future, riverboats and railroads lie ahead, and I fully intend to carry on in that direction. How does that sound?"

"Mr. Hartmann, I can't find a reason why I should not take that offer." David said with a smile.

"All right then," Mr. Hartmann replied, "Come in tomorrow morning and I'll find some desk space where you can work."

Anna and Chara were helping Little Jim pack his clothes, even though he told him he didn't need help. They had a piece of paper and a pencil for the purpose of making a list of things that he needed. The list only included his clothing. He was trying to think of other things he needed but he wasn't coming up with anything. It seemed really special that the two girls could write on a piece of paper, he asked them to read it for him.

"Pretty soon you gonna learn this too," Chara said, "now, here it says 'boots', see that's a 'b'. and two 'o's, and a 't'. Then 'stockings', then shirts."

"I can't think about learning that now, I got to think about horses and travelin.' I can't think about what I need besides clothes, maybe oilskins if it could rain, but I think the major worryin. about that," the boy said.

Anna Lee said, "Major gonna be takin' care of the food and all that. What about your hair, have you got somethin' to pick your hair with?"

"Oh, I don't need to do that for a few days," Jimmy replied.

"Maybe Mr. Brooks got a comb you could use," Chara Kee suggested, "or maybe Chester."

Maj. Thornton appeared in the doorway. "How's my jockey getting along, so far?"

"These two helpin' me make a list of what I need, sir. They think I need a comb for my hair."

The major smiled, "Well, we'll find one for you on our way to Hot Springs, my jockey needs to have his own. I've given it a lot of thought and have reached the conclusion that just Little Jim and I need to travel to Hot Springs. I'm leaving Chester in charge of the livestock and Brooks in charge of everything else. Are there any objections?"

Nobody said a word. "In that case," Big Jim asserted, "We'll leave in the morning right after breakfast.

Chester was up early. He went to the kitchen and found Mattie making biscuits. "Mornin' Miss Mattie, you ready for Mr. Brooks to be in charge for a few days?"

Mattie smiled, "Mr. Brooks in charge of the whole house except for the kitchen. I'm in charge of the kitchen. This kitchen gonna stay the way it always is- clean an' in order."

"I heard that, but who gonna keep them girls in line?" Chester asked.

"Them girls better stay in line, because sooner or later it's gonna be meal time an' if they want to eat they gotta have they work done."

"I know that's right, Miss Mattie, what would we do without you?"

"Well, you know," Mattie mused, "if for some reason, I can't do it, Chara and Anna do know how to cook, they spend a lot o' time in here and they seen me cook everything we eat."

When breakfast was ready, everyone was in the kitchen, including the major. Mattie had fixed grits and gravy and buttermilk to go with the biscuits and the coffee was hot and strong.

Little Jim asked, "Major, how we gonna eat while we gone?"

"Well, Mattie has packed up some food for us to take along on the trip. There are places along the way where we can sleep and have food to eat," Big Jim replied, "I realize you haven't ever been far from home while you were growing up, but the people we'll be seeing eat very much the same kind of food we do."

"That's good," Jimmy replied, "Is they a lot of folks where we going?"

"Well, let's see, there's a little settlement up ahead at the Sumacs. Then we'll go through Camden, then through some other small villages, before we come to a place called Arkadelphia. Then there will be another few small towns before we get to Hot Springs. So, we can expect to be seeing several hundred people, mostly strangers to us, before we get there," Big Jim related.

"Oh lord, that's a lot of people," Little Jim exclaimed. There were a few chuckles. "Is they all nice folks?"

"Most of them are. The folks in this part of the world are from many different places. Somehow or other we'll all have to get along. This will be new for you and myself too."

Chester asked, "Are y'all gonna take the buckboard, sir?"

"Yes, I think so, Chester. It will be easier to carry our clothes and what-not. I'm hoping the roads are good enough. Jimmy can ride Redbird and we'll let Mockingbird pull the buckboard."

"What if the roads are bad?" Chester asked.

"If the roads are bad we'll leave the buckboard somewhere for safe keeping and continue on horseback. In other words, it will take a lot to hold us back, right Jim?" The major said.

"Yes, sir, and we gonna win that race, Little Jim replied." The whole household laughed.

Little Jim said, "I just heard somebody holler. Sound like my mama, Pearl."

"I heard it too." said Brooks, "Look over yonder," he pointed to the east. Two horses were coming carrying five people. It was Miss Pearl and with Jimmy's two brothers and two sisters.

"Well, fine," Big Jim said, "let's let Jimmy say so long to his kin-folks, it is a long trip we're going on."

Little Jim's mother and siblings all dismounted and swarmed around him with kisses and hugs. Ivory and Essie Mary had taken up a collection in the black community and had two dollars and fifteen cents they'd raised to be wagered on Redbird to win. When the carriage was loaded and all the wishes and prayers were said, the major boosted the boy onto Redbird's back, then climbed into the driver's seat and clucked to the horse. "Hot Springs, here we come," Maj. Thornton announced.

The buckboard rattled along the road beside the river.

"What's this horse's real name?" Little Jim asked, "I can't remember what it is."

Maj. Thornton chuckled, "Most people who've heard it probably don't remember. It's 'Cardinal Archbishop'," he replied.

"Cardinal Archbishop, that's right, no wonder I couldn't remember,"the boy said, "What does that mean?"

"Well, in the old Catholic church, they have officials that are called cardinals. They wear red clothing and red hats. So a man named Audubon, who was giving names to our birds, saw our redbirds and named them 'cardinals'. When our sorrel colt was born, I wanted to name him 'Cardinal', but that name was already taken so I named him 'Cardinal Archbishop'. An archbishop is another old-time church official. Does that answer your question?"

"Yes, sir, I think so. I guess that's why we call him 'Redbird', it's easier to remember."

"That's exactly right. That's what nicknames are for, because they're easier to remember and pronounce," The major replied.

Jimmy said, "So what if he has colts of his own, what will their names be?"

"Oh I've thought of Scarlet Tanager, and Alizarin Angel," said Big Jim, "We'll just wait until they come along and then we'll find a name that suits the colt. What do you think?"

"Yes, I guess that's the way to do. Can I help you pick a name?" the boy asked.

"Sure you can, if you think of a good one, write it down, so you'll remember."

"Yeah, that's right, I'm learnin' my letters so I can write it myself. You know, this is gonna be fun," Jimmy enthused.

"I'll tell you what, my boy, I see you pulling back on that colt, trying to keep him in a trot. Mockingbird can't pull any faster than he's doing already, just let Redbird take a sprint for a ways, then come back and let us catch up."

Little Jim grinned, "Yes, sir," he said, and then turned loose on the reins. The big colt bolted into a full gallop and, within seconds he was very small to the major's eyes, and Big Jim felt his heart jump in his chest watching Redbird disappear in the distance.

When Little Jim and the Redbird returned the major told him how the sprint had lifted his spirits.

As they were nearing the place called 'The Sumacs' they

noticed a man sitting by the side of the road. As they drew nearer they could see he had a box sitting on the ground next to him. Big Jim called, "Whoa," and brought the buckboard to a stop. "Good morning, sir," the major said, "what are you selling?"

"Hens eggs," the man replied, "I live over to the west of here, among those big oak trees you can see."

"I'm not in the market for any eggs now, do you have any that are hard-boiled?" Big Jim inquired.

"No, sir, I don't, do you live near here?"

"I live just west of the town of West Creek, do you know of it?"

"No, sir, I don't, is it far?"

"It's only about six miles from here, you must be new in this area. West Creek has several hundred people living around it, if you were to bring your hens eggs and chickens to town on a Saturday, I'm sure you could sell some."

"That's good to know, sir, I'm Harold Foster and I've just moved here from Tennessee," the man replied."

The major said, "I'm Maj. James Thornton, and this is my hostler, Little Jim Sykes. Well, we must be going, we're on our way to Hot Springs."

"Good day to you, sir," Mr. Foster said, "You truly have some beautiful horses."

"Thank you," the Major replied, "and good luck on your chicken business, goodbye."

Another mile and they reached the Sumacs. "Them red berries is real pretty," Jimmy remarked, "do birds eat those?"

"I believe the redbirds and the mockingbirds eat those. Isn't that interesting, we've got one of each that are taking us to Hot Springs," Big Jim replied.

"I feel like our Redbird wants to take another sprint, sir, should I let him?" said Little Jim.

"By all means, let him run, but don't go too far, try to stay within my sight."

"Yes, sir," Jimmy replied as he gave his colt the reins; without a word Redbird was off at full speed. They repeated the 'sprint-and-return' process several more times with the sorrel horse never breaking a sweat. As the sun was dipping low on the horizon the road appeared more traveled. They were approaching Camden. There were fences on both sides of the road and the timber had been cleared for tillable fields.

"Are we stayin' here tonight?" asked Little Jim.

"Yes we are," the major replied, "Let's find the livery stable first, then we'll look for the hotel."

They headed for what looked like the town square. When they got there they went around it and soon located the stable. Camden was perched on a bluff over the Ouachita river. Looking down hill to the east they could see a boat-landing below. They stopped in front of the stable and a tall white man came out to meet them. He said, "Might you be Major Thornton front West Creek?"

"I am," Big Jim replied, "How did you know?"

"Word gets around," the man said with a smile, "I've been on the lookout for a big sorrel horse. I'm Phillip Nunn, at your service."

"Very well, sir," the major replied, "If you'll take care of these horses, the boy and I will walk over to the hotel."

"No rooms left at the hotel, big steamboats are at the landing. Right across the street is a rooming house run by Big Annie. She'll take care of you."

"All right then," Big Jim replied, "Let's get our bags and go see Big Annie."

Big Annie was a six foot tall white woman who weighed at least two hundred pounds. "Mr. Nunn knew you was coming, Major Jim, and who is this young-un?"

"This is Little Jim Sykes, he cares for my horses," the major responded.

Big Annie said, "We'll find you a room upstairs and Lunettie, in the kitchen has a place for Little Jim to stay. You all get settled in and supper will be ready directly. Lunettie soon appeared in the doorway; Annie told her to "Take Little Jim and show him where he'll be sleeping and then we'll all be ready to eat supper once the major's ready."

"Is there a table in the kitchen where we can all eat supper?" Big Jim inquired.

Big Annie chuckled, "If that's what you want, that's what we'll do, come on Major, I'll show you to your room."

Chapter 17

The sky was overcast as they left Camden. It was early morning as Big Jim drove the buckboard past the courthouse square and on up the road along the river. It seemed there were more than a few people standing in doorways and looking out of windows as they passed. He felt as though, perhaps, he and his tall sorrel colt and his jockey had drawn a certain interest among these simple agrarian people.
It was something new to them. It was new for Jimmy and Redbird as well. Jimmy looked hard in every direction, as if to penetrate the haze and look beyond the horizon. Redbird swung his head and puckered and flared his nostrils as if to catch every faint odor on the morning breeze. As the sun climbed higher, the haze cleared away and the cool spring day wrapped them in a gentle breeze that made the world seem fresh and new.

The major was thinking of his horse and his jockey. Would they do well? Only time would tell.
But even if they didn't, it wouldn't really matter. All that mattered was that they were chasing a dream in a way that most people never do. They were healthy and fit. He had a fine, big Thoroughbred colt, and a tough young rider. And together they were ready to take on anything the racetrack held in store for them.

The Sykes twins went to see Ira about the vines they had discovered across the river. "Well, boys, we got to think about this situation. When did you all get to thinkin' so much about muskydines?"

"We love 'em, Mr. Ira," Tyndall said, "they good for eatin' besides makin' wine. We went down and looked yesterday and they look like they turnin' into berries. Even if they just possum grapes, they be good for makin' jelly."

"Our mama Pearl make jelly from possum grapes that taste so good on biscuits," Wendell added, "If we had a bunch to make into jelly she'd be makin' a lot mo' biscuits."

"I know, I know," Ira said, "but I'm thinkin' what we need to do is use a telescope to look across the river."

"You got a telescope, Mr. Ira?" Tyndall inquired.

"No, I don't, but there must be somebody who does. Try to think of somebody who might have one. Maj. Thornton probably got one, but he's gone to Hot Springs. All right, let's go talk to Mr. Patterson."

Matthew was interested in what they had in mind. "Let's see, maybe two miles down the far bank of the river, are they- now what's the difference in these two grapes?"

"Muskydines is bigger. "Wendell asserted, "Takes a lot mo' possum grapes to make a mess o' juice, and it's got to be a secret."

"I understand," Matthew replied, "so the question is just taking a short trip down to find out what we've got. Well, this is what we can do, I'll take my white mare, one of you boys come with me, we'll make an exploratory venture down and back, and we'll know what we've got. How does that sound?"

"Yeah, yeah," the twins said simultaneously.

"Mr. Blacksmith, can you run us across the river?"

"I reckon so, I've seen you do it a few times."

Matthew flipped a coin to see which twin made the trip, Wendell won. They hitched the black horse to the windlass and led the white mare onto the flatboat. In fifteen minutes Matthew and Wendell were on the east bank. Matthew mounted up and pulled Wendell up in back of him.

In those days the understory of the forest was easy to walk through, before deforestation had caused the overgrowth by various bushes and vines. They stayed within sight of the river so as not to miss any of the vines they were looking for, which they expected to find in a natural clearing of some kind, where woody vines would have a good supply of sunshine. It took less than an hour do reach their destination. They were muscadines- they could tell from the larger size of the leaves. They were in a natural clearing where fallen trees and rocks had formed a space of about an acre and a half. They were nowhere near ripe, but the flowers were gone and the buds were in abundance.

"All right," Matthew asserted, "we've got a big secret to keep."

"We just hope nobody finds out," Wendell commented, "but it looks like there's enough here for a lot o' folks. Mr. Ira gonna make a lot o' wine this year."

After the haze had cleared it was a pleasant day as the major and his jockey made their way toward the Ouachita mountains. The sun was low in the sky when Jimmy asked his boss where they would stop for the night. "Well, Jimmy, it is about another twenty miles to Arkadelphia- I don't think we'll make it there at the pace we're moving. I hope we find a farmhouse or a lumber camp where we can retire. I know that horse has enough energy for another six hours, but the Mockingbird is getting tired."

They rode on for another eight miles and didn't see a farm of any size- mostly just forest. When they came around a bend in the river they saw a lumber camp up ahead. There were a dozen or so white tents in the area. Towards the middle of the camp there was a log building with a sign that read, 'saloon'. The major pulled up and climbed down from the buckboard. He told Jimmy to wait while he went inside to investigate. Big Jim entered the room, which was filled with lumberjacks who were drinking beer and singing. There was a man in a top hat seated at one of the tables. As he approached, the man looked up. "I am Maj. James Thornton from West Creek. I'm on my way to Hot Springs and it looks like I won't reach Arkadelphia. Do you know of a place I can spend the night?"

The man stood up. "I am Colonel Henry Lichtenberg, I supervise this camp. I'm sure I can find a place for you to spend the night. Are you traveling alone?"

"No, sir," Big Jim replied, "I have a thoroughbred horse and a colored jockey with me."

"Oh, I see," the colonel replied, "usually visiting horses stay in the corral with the mules, but a fine horse like that, we'll bring him out to my quarters where he can stay with my own horse. Would you accept my invitation to stay with us tonight?"

"If it's not too much of an imposition, I think I will. Actually I also have a another horse pulling my buckboard." Big Jim replied.

"Fine, fine, if I may ride with you, I'll show you to my domicile."

It was just turning dusk when the two men walked up to the wagon. "Jimmy, meet my friend Colonel Lichtenberg."

"Pleased to meet you, sir," Jimmy said.

"And this is your racehorse," the Colonel enthused, "what a fine looking animal. I presume he's going to race at Hot Springs. But we can discuss that on the way. Major, take the road to the top of the hill, Jimmy, just follow us my boy."

They had to stop a couple of times to remove logging

debris from the road, but they were there before it got dark. The Colonel was a veteran of the Confederate army. He had a wife and a daughter, and they had a live-in servant, Matilda, who did the cooking. Henry's wife was Julia and his teen-age daughter was Marigold. They had come from Alabama as had a number of people in the camp. Major Thornton slept on a settee in the front room and Jimmy slept in the kitchen on a palette on the floor.

The next morning, Little Jim was the first to rise. He slipped out the back door and went to check on the horses. The colonel's horse, along with the major's horses were standing, looking over the fence with, apparently, no hay to feed on. Jimmy quickly gathered up arms full of tall grass which he tossed over the fence for the horses. Soon the major was at the door. "Come on in Jimmy and have some breakfast."

When he came in the kitchen, Matilda said, "I hope you like biscuits."

"Oh I love biscuits, you got any jelly?" he replied.

"I got blackberry jam."

"Oh, I love that too. At home my momma makes muscadine jelly, it's the best, but blackberry is good too."

"So you gonna ride that big red horse in the races?"

"Yes, I am. His name is Cardinal Archbishop, but we call him Redbird. We gonna win too."

"Well I always heard, if you try your best, good things happen."

"Yes ma'am, that's true."

Soon it was time to travel north towards Arkadelphia. Col. Lichtenberg wouldn't hear of Maj. Thornton paying anything for his hospitality.
Even though they had fought on opposite sides in the war, they had a respect for each other. The Colonel asked him to stop in again when they returned home.

"What they do with all those trees, Major?" Jimmy wanted to know.

"First they make them into logs, then they saw them into boards. Then they can build houses, barns, even boats. Then, since they have cut the trees the land can be farmed." Big Jim explained.

"Who gonna live in all the houses and farm all the land?" Jimmy asked.

"Well back where I came from there are a lot of folks living very close together, and across the ocean, there are lot and lots of folks who want to come here and start a new life."

"Is they white folks or colored folks?"

"They are mostly white folks coming at this time, but someday, maybe a long time, but someday there will be be folks of all kinds- some tan, some yellow, some brown, as well as white and black, that will come here."

"I think I would like that," Jimmy said, "but it just seem like there's just so many folks, like I never seen all this time."

"And, there are many more a long way from here, and many will come here where it's not so crowded."

"Is that cause they don't wanna be so crowded?"

"No, it's because there isn't enough food, and they can move west and have land where they can farm."

"Oh, like the folks at home that they got some land where they can live on and farm."

"That's right, so they can grow food and raise a family."

"I think that's good," Jimmy opined.

"I think it's good too," the major replied.

As they traveled north it was apparent that they were going uphill; downhill at times, but it was a continuous increase in elevation. Around them there was a huge expanse of forest-mixed pine and deciduous trees.

"Is this the mountains?" Jimmy inquired.

"We're in the foothills of the Ouachita mountains, the way we're going, the mountains will get higher.
The roads will wind around through the hills to keep from having a too steep incline," Big Jim explained.

"The mountains look awful purty," Jimmy said.

"A lot of people would agree with you about that," the major replied. "We'll be coming to Arkadelphia soon, you can tell by the ruts that a lot of wagons have been up and down this road," the major mused.

"Why do they call it Arkadelphia?" Jimmy asked.

"Well, it means 'a city in Arkansas', which is what it is. It used to be called 'Blakelytown', which is hard to pronounce, so maybe they just wanted a prettier name that was easier to say," Big Jim suggested.

The natural beauty of the area was very noticeable. There were wildflowers in abundance- Indian paintbrush, crocus, and orange butterfly weed. Through the trees were white-blooming dogwoods, wherever the sun filtered through the upper story.

When they reached Arkadelphia they found it to be a thriving community, with many houses and businesses. Maj. Thornton saw a hotel near the town square and decided to stop there for a meal.

First he drove to the livery stable. It would probably not have been a problem to leave his horses tethered to a hitching post, but he didn't want to take the risk. He made sure to tell the stable man that these horses were highly valued and needed to have an eye kept on them. He made it a practice to give a little more money than was expected in return for better than average oversight.

As they walked back towards the hotel, Jimmy asked if the major knew if they treated colored jockeys well at the race track. "Well, my boy, at the present time there are a lot of colored jockeys working at the track. In fact, there may be more of them than white jockeys, however, we won't assume you won't encounter some shabby treatment. Believe me, I'll be watching close to see that we're respected," the major explained.

"I guess I need to go to the kitchen in the hotel, don't I?" Jimmy asked.

"Ah, yes, but I'll come with you to make sure the kitchen help know you're with me," said Big Jim.

The desk clerk asked Maj. Thornton if he would like a room. "No, thank you, I would like to dine with you though," Big Jim replied.

"Yes, sir, we would be glad to have you, dinner is fifteen cents, sir."

"Thank you, with your permission I'll conduct my helper to the kitchen so he can have dinner," said Big Jim.

The clerk said, "Down at the end of the hall on my left is the door to the kitchen- the cook is Mrs. Grassley, she will take care of your help."

Mrs. Grassley was a rotund white woman with a red apron and a big smile. The major said, " I am Maj. Thornton and this is my helper, Jimmy, I trust you can find him a place to eat while I'm having dinner."

"I certainly can, Major, just leave him to me. Is there anything else I can do for you?" she replied.

"Ah, yes, since you asked, we're on our way to Hot Springs, do you know if there is a settlement between here and there where we might spend the night?"

"Oh, yes, there is a small town about ten miles from Hot Springs known as De Roche. I'm from there myself. There is no hotel, but there is a rooming house where you can stay. Just tell them Ella Grassley sent you.

"Thank you kindly, ma'am, I will return for my helper a bit later," Big Jim told her.

While Major Thornton was eating, he reflected on how nice it would be if he could converse with his jockey while he was eating than have to raise his voice while they were traveling to speak to the boy.

The food was tasty, roast beef with rice and this odd green vegetable they called okra. There were two other guests at the table- a salesman who sold hand tools and the proprietor of the hotel who was also the desk clerk.

When Maj. Thornton was finished eating he went to collect his jockey. Jimmy was waiting at the door of the kitchen. "Did you enjoy your dinner," he asked.

"Yes, sir, that lady was real nice," said Jimmy.

As they walked to the livery stable, Jimmy talked about his meal in the kitchen. "Miss Grassley want to know if I been baptized. I told her I was, and she keep talkin' about how Jesus love us no matter who we is or where we live or anything about us."

The major said, "Yes, there are those people who live very close to their religion- it's always on their mind. They read their bible carefully and take it seriously. It may not be the same with all the Christians we meet, but at least for some, we can expect them to treat other folks fairly because they believe in that law of God that says, 'love your neighbor as yourself.'"

The stable man said, "You weren't gone long, sir. I fed them some corn and they ain't finished eatin' it yet."

Maj. Thornton thanked him and handed him a half-dollar and told him to keep the change. "Well, Jimmy, we're getting close, one more night on the road and the next day we'll be in Hot Springs."

"I never had such a good time in my whole life, Major," Jimmy mused, "I hope the food is just as good when we get there."

Big Jim said, "I've been told there is an eating place where all the cooking is done by colored folks. They fry chicken in hot lard, and they have mashed potatoes and hot biscuits at dinner every day. How does that sound?"

"Oh, lord," Jimmy replied, "makes me feel hungry just to hear about it."

The road became rocky and twisting, and, they felt as though they were climbing an incline at the same time. Very little sunlight was filtering down through the trees. Big Jim mused over the fact that people who were looking for land they could farm would feel like they were looking in the wrong place; maybe the ones who would find it appealing were from places in the old world which were hilly and densely forested- where they could build cabins from logs and be more isolated from the sight of other people. But this was just one stretch of road- climbing and twisting through dark woods, they would be glad to reach this place called De Roche while it was still daylight. They finally arrived just before the sun dipped below the horizon. A large white house was adorned with a sign that simply read, 'Rooming House.'

Maj. Thornton knocked on the front door. In a few minutes a white lady opened the door. "May I help you?" she inquired.

"My colored helper and I need a place to spend the night," Big Jim replied, "If you could oblige us, your house was recommended to us by Mrs. Grassley."

"Please come in. Yes, we have a room. Where is Ella living now?" she said.

"She is the cook in a hotel in Arkadelphia," the major replied, "You said you have one room?"

"Yes, do you mind having your helper stay in your room?" she asked, "We can bring a cot up to your room."

"I don't mind at all; let me find a place for my horses to spend the night and I'll be right back."

"Just lead them around to the back of the house, my husband, Mr. Clinton, will take care of your horses," she replied.

"Jimmy, help me lead these horses around back, the lady's husband will care for them. You don't mind sleeping on a cot in my room, do you?" the major said.

"Oh, no sir," he replied.

When they had reentered the house, Mrs. Clinton asked if they wanted some supper.

"Why, yes, ma'am, that would be fine," Big Jim replied.

"Well, when you're settled in, come back downstairs, "I've

got some cornbread, buttermilk, and turnip greens."

After they'd finished eating, they climbed the stairs to the guest room. "Major, can I ask you a question?" asked Little Jim.

"Certainly," the major replied.

"These white folks we been talkin' to, they seem different than the white folks down home. That's what it seem like."

"Well, Jim, the people down where we come from, lived in farm land all their lives, and all the colored folks used to be slaves. Now up in these mountains, there never were any colored folks until some of them came to Hot Springs with the white folks they work for, just like yourself and me. But all over these hills are white folks who never knew any colored folks. If we were to travel around up here, you would be the first black child they ever saw.
Now some of them would be scared. I know that seems strange, but it's really true. And some would just think, 'I've never been around any colored folks, I can't treat them any different than my own people.' Others would think, 'I don't know what these folks are like, I hope they stay away,'" the major explained. "Now in Hot Springs, there will be grooms and jockeys and most of them will be colored like you and Chester. They'll look at you and think, 'there's a jockey', see what I mean?"

"I think so sir, will folks be talkin' to me?"

"If they talk to you they'll be asking, 'which horse are you riding, and can he run?' You just tell them you're riding Redbird, and we'll find out how fast he can run when we get on the track. Which is all the truth they need to know."

Chapter 18

When Jimmy woke up he looked over at his employer and found him to still be sleeping. He was feeling a bit hungry. He put his clothes on and tiptoed down stairs to go check on the horses. The horses were awake, but apparently no one else was.

Mockingbird had a bit of mud on his legs, so he found a brush and used it to remove the mud. The horses were making rumbling sounds that indicated that they wanted to be fed. He would have to wait until Mr. Clinton showed up to attend to that. He kept thinking about what Big Jim had told him about the folks that lived in the mountains. He really had no idea how many people there were in these hills or how many miles of hills there were. It made him have a very lonely feeling, but if he were the first black child they had ever seen, he felt like he should make them not feel afraid. That was hard to think about since he couldn't imagine anyone being afraid of him. What could he do to them anyway?

He heard sounds coming from the house and imagined it was their landlady working in the kitchen. "Morning, Jimmy," Mrs. Clinton said as he entered the kitchen door, "You eat eggs?"

"Yes, ma'am," he replied, "I'll go see if the major's up."

Maj. Thornton was on his way downstairs at that very moment. When Jimmy saw him he said, "You eat eggs Major? Miss Clinton's fixin' eggs."

"Of course I do. I hope it's coffee I'm smelling," Big Jim replied.

As they walked into the kitchen Mrs. Clinton said, "No, Major, it's chicory. But I expect that when you reach Hot Springs they'll be serving coffee there."

"I hope so," the major replied, "although I won't turn down a cup of chicory when I get one."

Breakfast over, Maj. Thornton and Little Jim were back on their rocky, winding road. It was a clear day so it was fairly easy to see the wagon trail. Big Jim let the Mockingbird feel his way so he wouldn't have a misstep in the occasional rocks. It would have been very slow going if it had been a cloudy day. Almost before they realized it, the road leveled off so it wasn't so much of an incline. Gradually they came into open country. There were a few farms along the road and there were signs that more wagons had been up and down this road.

"We're approaching Hot Springs, Jim," the major said, "you probably figured that."

"Yes, sir," the boy replied, "how far is it to the race track?"

"I'm not sure where it is. There is a Col. Fordyce that has built a hotel known as the Arlington. It is in the center of town. We'll make that our destination for the time being. In the meantime we'll have an eye open for racing activities. Since the end of the war, Hot Springs has been growing quite rapidly and thus, changes are constantly happening. I believe that the racing has been going on in an area to the south and east of the city. As we draw closer to the hotel I mentioned, we'll find out more."

"Is folks comin' here because of the hot water?" Jimmy asked.

"That's right," Big Jim replied, "the word has spread all over the country that the hot water from the springs has healing power. Folks with all kinds of ailments are coming here in hopes of finding a cure for whatever ails them. I believe that they are racing horses because folks need some kind of entertainment while they seek their cure. Now, in addition to racing, we can expect to see a good deal of drinking and gambling going on as well. You and I, we'll just attend to our own concerns and pay no mind to what else goes on."

"But the folks is gamblin' on the horses ain't they?" Jimmy asked.

"Yes, that's part of the appeal, the attraction, of racing is to wager their money," the major replied, "and I dare say, that's what I'm doing as well. I'll risk some money, no more than I can afford to lose, and, if we win, I'll make money, and that horse you're riding will be worth more, and I can charge more money for his breeding fee."

"That's a whole lot o' things to think about," Jimmy replied, "'cause you gonna be countin' on me to do it right."

"Well, it's just like we've talked about since you came to work for me, if he breaks out fast, hold on to him just a little until you see if he's ready to gain on the other horses, then let him know it's time to run." the major explained, "do you feel like you can do that?"

"Yes, sir, I do," Jimmy said with a smile.

"All right, then," Big Jim said, "We're ready to race."

As they proceeded toward the center of town they encountered many people walking, riding horses, and traveling in carriages. There were quite a number of both black and white people; a few that looked like they were Native American, and a few that didn't fit in any of those categories. Their clothing was in many different styles. Some of the white people were almost formally dressed, but most of them wore working-class clothes. Most of the black people wore very plain work clothes, but some wore uniforms, that were related to the places where they worked, but the uniforms gave them an appearance of respectability. Little Jim's collarless white shirt and gray pants looked more like the working class, but his high-topped boots with the pants tucked inside gave him more the look of the uniformed black people.

There were buildings of all descriptions in every direction. There were brick buildings, and buildings made of natural stone. There were wood buildings of all varieties. Some were stately frame structures with clapboard siding. There were buildings made of unfinished logs, and there were many made of unfinished lumber which could only be described as shacks, and there were lots of tents- some of them just makeshift.

They saw a sign that told them they were on Valley Street. They were stopped at an intersection by a man dressed in what looked like a blue military uniform. It seemed he was directing traffic. A young white boy approached them and asked, "Are you folks looking for a stable?"

"Why, yes, we are," the major replied, "which direction is it?"

"Just follow me," the boy replied. He headed east, to the right of the street, with Big Jim and Little Jim in tow. They traveled about a quarter mile- then turned right down an alley. The stable was larger than any of the stables where they had stopped on their trip. The proprietor emerged from a small shack. Major Thornton stepped to the ground. Holding out his hand he said, "I am Major James Thornton from West Creek Arkansas- this is my hostler, Little Jim Sykes."

"Glad to meet you, Major," the man said, taking his hand "I'm Johnny Moran." He handed the white boy a penny and said, "Go find some more, Danny."

Jimmy dismounted and held Redbird by the reins.

"Are we near the racetrack, Mr. Moran?" the major inquired.

"Yes, sir, the Fairground is a half mile east of here. If you're requiring a place to board your horses between there and bathhouse row, you've come to the right place. I charge ten cents a day for one horse. Since you have two animals I'll charge you fifteen cents a day."

Maj. Thornton nodded his approval. "The sorrel colt is a fine looking animal," Moran observed, "Will you be racing him here?"

"That is my intention, perhaps you can tell me where I can find Col. Warren," the major inquired.

"His office is right by the Fairground, you might find him there." Moran informed him.

"Are we goin' to the Fairgrounds, Major?" Jimmy asked.

"No, Jim, let's go to the hotel first, we've got plenty of time," Big Jim told him. He paid Mr. Moran for two days board for the horses, then they took their bags in hand and headed for Valley Street. There was a tall building that was prominent in view in the distance, and Big Jim knew it must be the Arlington Hotel. It was far enough that the major hailed a carriage-for-hire and he and Jimmy rode to the hotel. The front of the hotel had a columned porch from one end to the other. There was a broad stone staircase with large stone columns on each side. There were uniformed black men standing at each side of the entrance. When Big Jim and his jockey stepped out of the carriage, one of the men quickly arrived to help them with the luggage. As they climbed the steps, the major said to the doorman, "I've heard there is an eating place near here that is operated by colored folks, do you know where it is located?"

"Do I know where it's at?" he replied. Big Jim nodded. "You go down the hill 'til you get to Malvern Road and turn left. You'll see it on the right side of the street, it's called 'Velma's Smoke House', it's the best food in town."

They paused at the top of the steps. The major spoke to the doorman again, "We're new in town, what's the hotel's policy about colored helpers?"

The doorman said, "Well, sir, he can stay in your room but he would have to stay in the room the whole time. What I would do, if it was me, they could find him a place to stay down at the smoke house, while you're in town. Tell Velma that Leon sent you."

The major asked Jimmy, "Would you like to stay at the Smokehouse or would you rather stay with me?"

"Oh, I'll be fine down at the Smokehouse."

They entered the hotel lobby and approached the desk. "I'm Maj. Thornton, and I'd like a room for three days, and, by the way, is Col. Fordyce in the vicinity?"

"The Colonel is rarely here, sir, he may be in St. Louis, we never know until we hear from him" the desk clerk explained, "Is he a friend of yours?"

"We both served in the cavalry, he in Ohio, myself in Kentucky. I thought it would be nice to meet him if I had the chance." Big Jim said.

The clerk asked, "Will your help be staying here as well?"

"No, he has accommodations elsewhere."

The clerk said, "If you will sign the register, the room is fifty cents a night. You'll be staying in room ten, up one flight of stairs."

The Major turned to Jimmy, "If you'll wait here with Leon, I'll run up to my room and be right back."

Jimmy walked back out to hotel porch.

Leon asked, "How long you been working for that man?"

"Two years now," Little Jim replied, "He got a big fine three-year-old colt, we gonna race him at the fairgrounds."

The doorman smiled, "And you the jockey?"

"Yes, sir" said Little Jim.

"Well that's fine, that's just fine. You probably the youngest jockey in the race." said Leon.

The major soon returned. "Well, Jim, let's saunter on down to this dining establishment and see what's on the bill of fair. Leon, thanks for your help," he said as he handed Leon a dime.

"Thank you, sir," the doorman responded as they descended the steps. Jimmy put his clothes sack over his back and walked down the street with the major.

In ten minutes they were at Velma's. It was three in the afternoon. The man who answered the door said, "May I help you, sir?"

Maj. Thornton said, "My jockey and I would like some food and I'd like to speak with Velma."

The man said, "I'll be your waiter, my name is Walter," he pointed to a table, "please sit down and I'll get Velma to come talk with you."

"Thank you, tell her that Leon at the Arlington

recommended her." the major replied.

Walter returned with glasses of water, napkins and silverware. "Miss Velma will be here directly. All we can offer you is leftover from the noon hour, but we have baked ham, black-eyed peas, okra, turnip greens, rice and gravy, and I believe we have a few pieces of fried chicken."

Big Jim said, "Bring this boy the chicken, and I'll have a slice of ham."

Walter said, "Fine, I'll bring you bowls of vegetables and you can help yourself."

Velma arrived and introduced herself. "So Leon told you about us."

Big Jim said, "Please sit down, I am Maj. Jim Thornton from West Creek and this is my horse-handler, Little Jim Sykes." Velma sat down at the table. "I need a place for Jim to stay while we're in town. He's going to ride my horse in the races on Sunday afternoon."

"Little Jim can stay here with us. I have a bunk room in the back where he can sleep." Velma said.

Walter arrived with their food. He said, "All we had left of the chicken was a wing and a drumstick.
You need to eat with us tomorrow when the chicken is fresh out of the pan."

Jimmy bit into the drumstick while Walter served him rice and gravy. They didn't need to ask him how it tasted, they could tell from the look on his face that it was heavenly. Besides the vegetables there was a plate of biscuits and butter.

"Well, I'll leave you folks to your dinner, "Velma said, "is there anything else I can do for you?"

"Well, yes," the major began."It's about this boy's hair...."

"Oh, yes, I know what you need to do, there's a barber shop for colored just down the street, they'll take care of him," said Velma. "Ask Walter to point it out to you after you're finished eating."

They left Jimmy's clothes sack in the bunk room. The barber shop was just a short walk away. It had the obligatory red-and-white striped pole and it also had a sign that read, 'for colored' and included a silhouette of a black man. It smelled of soap and pomade inside. Jimmy looked around in wonderment of this place which was dedicated to beautifying curly black hair. "Can we help you sir?" the barber inquired.

"Jimmy, tell the man what you want," the major coaxed.

The barber laid a thick cushion in his big chair and said, "Step over here son and tell me how you'd like it done."

Little Jim climbed into the chair and looked around at his image in the mirror. His curly hair was a little stringy and rather uneven. There were a few pictures on the wall of different hair styles. He pointed at one that looked short, but not too short. "Like that one I guess."

The barber said, "All right, let's wash it first, then we'll trim it."

Big Jim sat down in an armchair to witness the proceedings. The barber wrapped a cloth around Jimmy's neck and sprinkled water from a bottle onto his head, then he poured some shampoo into his hands a worked Little Jim's hair into a lather.

After rinsing it and toweling it dry, he took a large toothed ivory comb and began pulling out on Jimmy's hair. Soon it was very fluffed out. He took a pair of shears and trimmed all around- stretching the curls out with the comb and snipping off the ends.

Big Jim asked, "Have you got a comb like that you can sell us?"

"Not like this one," the barber replied, "this one came all the way from Africa. But I have one made of maple wood that's very good. I'll show it to you when I'm done with this boy's hair."

Jimmy's hair had never looked so good. He smiled as he turned his head from side-to-side looking in the mirror. "Now I'll show you that comb," the barber said.

"Show it to the boy," the major said. The barber handed it to Jimmy. It was light brown and very shiny- about four inches wide with teeth about two inches long. Jimmy turned it over in his hand and ran his fingertips over the teeth. He smiled at his boss.

"I guess he likes it," Big Jim said, "What do we owe you?"

"I need to get twenty-five cents for the comb and the haircut is five cents, so thirty cents."

Big Jim handed him a half-dollar and said, "Keep the change." The barber smiled.

The major said, "Well, lets go check on our horses, Jim, what do you say?"

"Yes, sir, that's a good idea. Thank you for the haircut."

"Ah, ha, I've never seen you look so good, got your comb?"

"Right here in my pocket, it'll keep my hair lookin' nice." It was just a short walk to the stable. Mr. Moran was standing at the gate.

"Your boys is fine, Major. Fed them some corn. That Mockin'bird gets real upset if you get between him and the Redbird."

Maj. Thornton said, "Well they're close friends, you know." Moran chuckled. "Say, Jimmy will be dropping by from time to time to check on them. He's staying at Velma's Smokehouse. If there's any problems just knock on Velma's back door and let him know, all right?"

"I'll do that, and just so you'll know, either Danny or myself will always be here. We never go off and leave them horses unwatched," said Mr. Moran.

"So don't be surprised if Jimmy comes by from time to time," the major added.

"Right sir, and we'll look to find him at Velma's," Moran replied.

"Thank you sir," said Big Jim, "Jim, let's walk on over to the Fairgrounds and have a look at it."

The major decided to go by way of Malvern Road- the location of most of the black businesses in Hot Springs. There were hotels, saloons, cafes, and gaming houses. The gaming places offered billiards, checkers, and dominoes- all of which could be played with wagering involved. In fact, everything that was available to whites, except bathing, was available to blacks on 'Black Broadway', which was Malvern Road. Bathing for colored folks was to be found at the public bath house which was administrated by the National Park Service.

The Fairgrounds were mainly just a broad expanse of pasture land surrounded by stately oak trees. There were some simple unpainted frame buildings that looked like they were being used to stable horses. The major looked around to see if he could find Col. Warren's office. He noticed that the last building they had passed was a saloon on Malvern Ave. He said to Little Jim, "Unless I missed my guess, I think I see Col. Warren's office. They headed in that direction. As they entered the room they saw a well-dressed gentleman at a table playing solitaire.

"Col. Warren, I presume," the major said, doffing his hat.

"Ah, yes," the man replied, "and you are?"

"Major James Thornton, and this is my jockey, Little Jim

Sykes."

"Splendid," Col. Warren said, "I've been expecting your team to arrive. Please sit down."

"Well, you're seeing our entire team," Big Jim replied as he and Jimmy sat down, "the two of us- my colt is at Mr. Moran's stable at the present time."

"A good fellow, Johnny Moran, we're good friends," the colonel mused, "I have your entry form close by, I'll fetch it so you can witness it after I sign it." The colonel rose and walked over and entered a room and then returned with a sheet of paper in his hand. He placed it on the card table and signed it, then the major signed his name below it.

"I believe your horse is the last entry in the race," the colonel stated, "with yours there will be eight horses in the field. The largest field we've had for opening day since I've been here. Tell me more about your colt, sir."

"He's registered with the Jockey Club by the name 'Cardinal Archbishop', he is of Kentucky breeding, tracing back to the Darley Arabian."

"Splendid, may I buy you a drink," the colonel offered.

"Thank you, but no,"said Big Jim, "it's late and we're tired, perhaps in the morning we can drop by."

"Yes, of course," said the colonel, "remember, the race will be on Sunday at two o'clock."

"Fine," Big Jim replied, "We'll see you then."

The two Jims made their way back to Moran's stable and found Danny in charge. He told them that Moran had gone around the corner for a drink.

"Is he your father then?" Big Jim inquired.

"Yes he is," Danny replied.

"You're Irish then," the major said, "Tell me, is there a Catholic church in Hot Springs?"

"Not truly, sir, Father O'Rourke, says Mass at the train depot- the trains don't run on Sunday" Danny replied."

"I see," said Big Jim, well keep an eye on these horses, we'll see you tomorrow."

"Yes, sir, good night."

As they made their way up Valley St., Jimmy asked the major why the Catholics would meet in the train depot. "There aren't many Irish or Italians in the area so they haven't built their own church. The depot isn't being used by the railroad on Sunday, so they hold their service there. But there are a great many Irish and Italian people back east and across the ocean who will be coming west some day. Those folks will all be Catholic. Then, I'm sure they'll have their own church."

Jimmy asked, "Is Mr. Patterson a Catholic?"

"I'm sure he must be, but he's the only one I know of," said Big Jim.

"He's a real nice man, Major. He told Mama if she ever need any help, just come get him."

"He is a nice man, Jimmy, we're lucky to have him in our town."

They knocked on the back door of the Smokehouse and Velma answered it. "Come on in here, boy, we fixin' to have supper. Major you want to eat too?"

"Thank you ma'am, but I need to get back to the hotel."

"Well let me fix you a sandwich to take with you," she said. In a few minutes she handed him a sandwich wrapped in a napkin. "Just bring the napkin back, please."

"Thank you ma'am, I will," the major said as he headed for the Arlington.

Velma said, "You know, Jimmy, that's the only white man ever called me 'ma'am'."

Chapter 19

When Major Thornton was back in his room he poured himself a glass of water and sat down in a chair to eat his sandwich. It was smoked pork on white bread- a little sweet, a little spicy, but very good. He took a sip of the water. He could taste a hint of dissolved minerals, but it was not very different from average well-water. He took out a pad of paper and began making notes of the day's occurrences. A knock came at the door. He stood and opened the door. It was a well-dressed gentleman in a top hat. The man said, "Maj. Thornton?" as he held out his hand.

"Why, yes," said Big Jim, taking his hand.

"I am Col. Sam Fordyce."

"Well, come in and sit down, I didn't expect to see you." the major said.

The colonel said, "I came into town for the first day of the racing season and they told me you were in the Kentucky Cavalry. I served in the Ohio Cavalry, and after the war I moved to the South and began building railroads."

"And hotels and bathhouses, I gather."

"Yes, and I want to build an opera house. One sees a need and tries to supply it. I felt that the thermal springs needed to be federally administered and I've been trying to persuade the War Department to build a hospital here. But come let me show you around the hotel and offer you some refreshment." Big Jim agreed and they entered the hall and descended the staircase to the ground floor. "How about Kentucky bourbon, Major?" They entered the barroom and sat down at a table. When the waiter arrived the colonel said "Two bourbons in tall glasses with ice."

When the drinks arrived neither man said anything for several minutes, then Col. Fordyce said, "Well, Major, allow me to show you around my hotel. It's not only my hotel, I have two partners. With three partners we can each be looking after his own interest, which is also the group interest. I don't intend to stay here all the time, so we each have some leverage- if you see what I mean."

Big Jim said, "I think I do, sir, please go on."

"Let's climb the stairs to the upper story and then we can leisurely descend." From the third level they could view the bathhouses and the mountain, unobstructed to the

Northwest. From the other side of the building they could see the natural open area where the track was located, and also the railroad coming from the Southeast. "The structure is based on Italian Renaissance architecture. I intended to make it look to be the 'best' hotel here. Now tell me about yourself, Major."

"Well I too had a fondness for the Southland. I have one child, a son. My wife died much too young before I came to Arkansas. I acquired a piece of land in Union County- right near the Louisiana border and bought some quality Thoroughbred horses. I have a colt I am racing on Sunday, my first venture into the racing business." the major explained.

"Is your son involved as well?" asked the colonel.

"No, he wants to make a career in the shipping business, and he's working in New Orleans at the moment," the major responded.

"I trust he's aware of the future in the railroads," Col. Fordyce commented.

"He is, he's trying to stay informed of all the rail building enterprises in this part of the world." said Big Jim.

"There is a great deal of growth going on, and it will continue for the foreseeable future. However, there is something to consider; there are those who have the engineering skill and those who have the business skill, and the two skills do not necessarily coincide. There will be a great deal of activity and not all of it will be successful. But, I can assure you, any track that gets laid, will eventually become part of a network- just like roads and canals. Impress upon your son these basic facts, because if he is aware of this, he will certainly succeed, even though others may fail. But what of you own enterprises?"

"Excuse me a moment Colonel, what you've just told me has had such an impact on my thought process that I must take a moment and let it all sink in," Maj. Thornton managed, "allow me to jot down a few things to remember."

The colonel chuckled, "Of course, it's refreshing to speak with someone who pays attention to what I'm saying." Big Jim wrote down 'engineering' and 'management' and 'network'.

"All right, Colonel, I think I've got it."

"Please, just call me Sam."

"And just call me Jim. Yes, my colt is a Kentucky bred

animal. Bloodlines that go back to the Darley Arabian. I have a negro jockey, fourteen years old, who's smart and tough. His name is also Jim- I call him Little Jim. My whole household is negro since my son moved to New Orleans. One man, Chester manages my livestock, the rest take care of the house. Just my jockey and I came here from Union County."

"Did you come by rail from Malvern?" the colonel wanted to know.

"No, I wasn't certain about all the particulars involved." the major replied.

"Yes, of course," said Sam, "If you could secure a boxcar, that would provide room for two or more animals with feed plus an attendant. I'll have to look into providing that kind of service. Even as we speak there are wealthy folks around the country building private rail cars. When we have a network of railroads, and we shall, the private cars can be coupled on to a train going anywhere there are rails, and be laid off on a sidetrack, while the owners disembark to visit and sight-see to their hearts content, then come home or travel on as they wish."

"That's sounds fantastic," Jim replied, "But it's all going to happen."

"You bet it is," Sam Fordyce responded. "Now, since you and your jockey are new in town, I'll let you in on some of the peculiarities of this area. There are people here from all over and from all walks of life. First of all, there are the throngs of folks who come here for treatment for their ailments. Some have a good deal of money, some have very little. Then, there are those who are here to make money. Many of them are just small business people or laborers. In addition to those there are the ones out to get rich quick, and they can be dangerous. There is cheap low grade liquor, there are gamblers, there are houses of prostitution. No resort area could expect to be free of that element. But be wary of the sharpers and bunko artists who are out to defraud. If it is one thing Hot Springs is lacking in, it is effective law enforcement."

"I thank you for that information. Well, I've had a very busy day," Jim stated, "and I really need to get some rest. Thanks so much for your hospitality and your sound advice about the shipping business."

"By all means, let me walk you back to your room," said

the colonel.

When Big Jim bid goodnight to Col. Fordyce he sat down and made some notes about what the man had told him. He knew it would be very helpful to David. He thought about what a coincidence it was that he and the Colonel had such a similar story. He also thought about his employee and hoped that things were going well. It seemed good fortune that Little Jim was bunked in close to the stable where he could keep a close watch on their horses. It occurred to him that the boy might have a false sense that people here were kinder than in West Creek. But then, he was close to local colored folk who would surely keep him apprised of the realities they faced.

Jimmy didn't feel confidant about going out after dark, but he had told Big Jim he would. He didn't know what time it was and it appeared that everyone in Velma's place was asleep- except for him. This place was all strange to him. So he ran it over in his mind. Get out of bed, put his pants on, don't need the boots, walk out the back yard, cross the street. Just one step at a time- well, one thing at a time, the steps would be one at a time too. He sat up, reached for the pants, stood up, one leg, the other leg, he felt easier already. This wouldn't take but a few minutes, then he could go back to bed. He walked towards the door and felt for the knob. His hand on the knob, he opened the door and looked out. It was really dark. He stepped out and closed the door. He heard a faint sound of music and voices. There must be saloons that were open. Then he could see a little better, but not enough to see the ground. It occurred to him that if anyone came around here and tried to do anything to these horses they would need to have a torch, and if they had a torch, he would easily see them. That made sense. He felt his way to the street, stepped on the hard ground and walked to the other side. Then he turned left and started moving in that direction. Soon he was able to make the odor of horse manure. Then he found the gate to the stable. No one was up. He crawled between the slats and into the passageway. Redbird was three stalls down on the left. Mockingbird was in the next stall. When he got to Redbird, the horse was standing. Sometimes they sleep standing up. He looked at Mockingbird, who was lying on his side. He was sure they were all right. Then he heard a voice, "Is that you Jimmy?" It was Danny. "Yeah, it's me, just checking on the horses."

"Yeah, they're all right, I just checked myself," Danny replied.

Little Jim said, "Guess I'll go back and get some sleep. Sure is dark."

"Ain't no moon tonight," said Danny, "Well, lets go get some sleep. Goodnight."

"Yeah, goodnight." Jimmy reversed his steps back to Velma's. He'd done what he told the major; he'd checked on the horses.

He woke in the morning to the smell of bacon and coffee. He knew it was real coffee- he had smelled it often enough at Darley Hill. And he knew Big Jim would be happy. He started dressing. This time he needed his boots. His socks weren't completely dry and he had a hard time slipping his boots on. When he had all his clothes on he made a trip to the outhouse. By the time he returned he could hear his employer's voice in the dining room. "Miss Velma, you knew what I wanted."

Velma giggled, "A gentleman deserves to have a strong cup of coffee."

"And here's your napkin, ma'am."

Big Jim and Little Jim sat down to a sumptuous breakfast. "Did you visit the horses, Jim?" the major inquired.

"Yes, sir, it was real dark. I got to thinkin', if anybody came around they would need a torch to see, and if they had a torch, I would see them before they could see me." Jimmy said.

"That's quite true, young man, you've got a good mind," the major allowed. "I met a famous man last evening, Col. Samuel Fordyce."

"Does he own Hot Springs?" Jimmy asked.

"Not entirely, but he owns more of it than anyone else does. He built a hotel, a bathhouse, and the railroad, and he saw to it that this is a National Park. It would certainly be a different place if he hadn't come here."

"Is he your friend?" Jimmy asked.

Big Jim chuckled, "Yes, I'm happy to say, I think he's our friend, and we couldn't find a better person in the state of Arkansas to have as a friend. Now, what do you say, after we finish breakfast, we'll saddle our horses and wander around this town for a while."

"I say, that's a good idea. Do you want to ride Redbird?" asked Jimmy.

"No, you ride him. I don't want to give him any doubts about who he's carrying. I'll ride the Mockingbird," said the major. They saddled the two horses and the major lifted Little Jim onto Redbird. "Let's trot down to the fairground so we can lope around the track." Once Big Jim was mounted they headed down Malvern Road. Lots of folks were out on the sidewalks and many of them turned their heads as the two riders passed. They could see which way they were heading and Big Jim thought he saw several follow them down towards the fairground. The track was a simple oval- it looked to be a mile and a half. There was an outer rail that consisted of posts, twelve feet apart, with planks nailed to the tops. Then there was an inner oval of the same construction with another row of planks on the upper inside in addition to the ones on top. The distance between the outer and inner rail was wide enough to accommodate ten horses.

The major and his jockey casually entered the track through an open side gate and walked their horses to where the backstretch would be during a race. They stopped and stood there for a minute or two. Finally they started into a lope, and then a gallop, going counter-clockwise around the oval. Jimmy didn't let him stay at a dead run, just long enough to give him a feel for what was going to happen the next afternoon.

Having given the sorrel colt some good exercise, they settled down into a trot, then a walk before they headed back toward Valley Street. When they reached Orange St. they turned and headed towards Hot Springs Mountain. As they passed an alley, Big Jim noticed a crap game going on, on the hard dirt surface. They could be shooting dice anywhere in the country just as easily, but some sharper with a pair of loaded dice could be earning his living from all the tourists in the spa resort. Jimmy noticed a pair of men walking up the street carrying what looked like chickens under their arms. He asked the major why two men would be carrying chickens on the street. "Well, son, they have rooster fights with a prize to the winning rooster. Besides that, lots of side bets can be made."

There were well-dressed women with low-front bodices carrying parasols. It was evident that they had something they were offering for sale. They turned left on Prospect Avenue and rode south along the edge of the mountain. It seemed there were several well-dressed young women strolling along Prospect Avenue. Big Jim wondered if this was someone's idea of having a designated area for a certain type of business transaction- like having saloons or gambling halls in a certain area.

When the sun was straight up in the sky they headed for Velma's for dinner. Along with the usual bill of fair there was freshly baked corn bread and sweet 'tater pie.

Chapter 20

Back in West Creek, Ben Tilton was making some pills that Dr. Biggs had prescribed for Miss Baxter, a twenty-eight year old daughter of Tom Baxter, a local farmer. Helen Baxter was sitting in a chair by the door and going through her handbag, trying to locate a silver dollar that she knew was in there- she just didn't know where. "I know I've got a dollar in here somewhere, Ben," she said.

"Perhaps you'd like to empty your bag on the counter, it might be easier," the druggist replied.

"I think I will," said Helen. She set her bag on the counter and started removing and laying items on the surface- a fountain pen, a watch, a comb, a tin of powder, a round rock the size of a bird's egg.

"What's that?" Ben inquired.

"Which?"

"That rock."

"Oh that's my lucky stone. It's a piece of clear gravel I found out in the cotton field in Chicot County when I was a child." Helen said.

"May I look at it?" Ben asked.

"Of course," she replied. Tilton picked up the stone and felt the surface. He fetched a metal stylus and drew the tip across the surface, then looked for a scratch. There was none.

"I'm going to weigh this ma'am." he said.

"As you wish," Helen replied.

Ben placed the stone on one side of his balance, then started adding weights to the other side. When the sides were balanced he said, "Whew, seven grams, about a quarter of an ounce."

"Is it something valuable?" Miss Baxter wanted to know.

"Well, if it is what I think it is, it could be very valuable." Mr. Tilton said.

"What do you think it is?" she asked.

"I think you have a diamond. The biggest one I've ever seen," he replied, "I think you should get it appraised."

"How would I do that?" she asked.

"You would have to have it looked at by a jeweler or a diamond broker. I'm not sure where there is one."

"Mr. Tilton, does this mean there are diamonds around where I found this?" Helen asked.

"Well, no, I don't think so, but there are a lot of diamonds in Africa, and one of the slaves probably brought this over here. They might not have known what it was- just their lucky stone they carried around with them, just like you." Ben told her.

After a few moments she said, "I wonder whose it was."

"Well, it belongs to you now; you have it in your possession. Listen, if I were you, I wouldn't say anything about it to anyone, and I'll do the same." he said, "It's just between us, and in the meantime I'll find out where it can be appraised. So just put it back in your bag and I'll get your pills for you. You know, it's really enigmatic when you pause to think about it. All those people being rounded up and forced into slavery, when there were precious stones all around there, that were worth far more than their manual labor would ever produce."

"Yes, when you think about it, it is rather curious."

Maj. Thornton and Little Jim were riding south along Prospect Ave. when they saw a young blue jay on the ground under a tree. Jimmy wanted to dismount and look at it, so the major held Redbird's reins. As Little Jim bent down to look at the bird, all of a sudden an adult bluejay swooped down and ricocheted off his head. "Aaah, leave me alone, I won't hurt him," he cried.

The major chuckled, "Best leave him alone, she won't let you get close to it."

"Did she do that 'cause I'm colored," Jimmy asked.

"No, no, she would've done the same to anyone. A bird wouldn't be smart enough to know you might be trying to help, she would have attacked anyone or any thing what got close to her baby." Big Jim explained.

Well, I'll never do that again," Jimmy replied.

They turned back southward and walked their horses toward Valley Street. As they approached the intersection they heard the sounds of drumming and whistling. It was a pair of colored men, one with a drum and one with a fife, entertaining a small group of tourists. The drum played a cadence 'boom, boom-boom, boom, boom-boom', while the fife played 'Tweet, tweetle-tweet, tweet, tweetle-tweet.' Then the drum played alone for several minutes. Then they stopped playing and the crowd applauded. There was a hat lying in the street, brim up. Every so often, someone would toss some coins into the hat. When they started again, the drum played a long roll while the fife played Scotland the Brave. The major glanced over at Jimmy, he appeared to be really enjoying the music. He dismounted and then held Redbird's reins so the boy could dismount. Little Jim was grinning. Maj. Thornton found a quarter in his pocket and handed it to the boy so he could throw it in the hat. It was probably the biggest tip they got all day, but he felt like they deserved it since most people couldn't give anything.

They left the street musicians and headed in the direction of Johnny Moran's. The matter of making wagers on the race was at hand since racing would be the next day. Moran told them it would be advisable to make the bets through a third party and he recommended a man by the unlikely name of Johnny Jones. Since Moran was acquainted with Jones, the major let him deal with the other John, for a ten percent cut, which seemed reasonable. Jim Thornton handed the stakes, which amounted to twenty-five dollars, over to Moran and he and Danny went to make the transaction. In a few minutes, Danny returned to ask if five to one would be acceptable. Maj. Thornton eagerly accepted since he would have settled for two to one.

When Moran returned he seemed amused. It seemed that the bookmakers thought it was unlikely that a horse from south Arkansas stood any chance of winning a race. "These folks are known to place big bets on races without ever looking over the horses they are so certain will win or lose. But that's why 'tis a money making process for those who really know horses." Maj. Thornton didn't ask him if he had bet any of his own money on Redbird.

"Well, young man," Major Thornton said to Jimmy, "I have a mind to eat an early supper, and turn in early. Tomorrow is Sunday, but I don't know of a church that would welcome us both."

"The AME church where miss Velma goes would welcome us, she told me that. Their church is just a block down on Malvern Road from the Smoke House," said Little Jim.

"Well, why not, any port in a storm," Big Jim replied, "if they'll have me, I'm sure Jesus would approve."

They rode back to Moran's and unsaddled their horses. Jimmy and Danny led them to their stalls and fed them some corn. Johnny had gone around the corner to Shaughnessy's saloon for a drink. The saloon was a gathering place for working class men. There was an upright piano in the corner being played by a man named Chunky, who also played the piano at the Methodist church. He knew most of the songs written by Stephen Foster, but his favorite song was Golden Slippers. The men in Shaughnessy's were discussing the next day's racing. Johnny heard the name Bald Eagle mentioned several times. He gathered that the horse in question was a bay with a 'bald' face that was owned by a man named Charles Eagle. Apparently several men considered him a favorite to win. There was a man named Dick Decatur who had placed all the money he had, twelve dollars, on Bald Eagle. All this talk about Cardinal Archbishop was making him nervous. As he sipped his beer and listened to the piano, he couldn't get his mind off of the race on Sunday. He knew he wouldn't be able to sleep unless he had some assurance that Baldy had a chance to win that race. As he thought about it, a scheme began to grow in his mind. He remembered that in the back of Johnny Moran's was a corral where sometimes carriages owned by Johnny's customers were kept while their horses were being cared for by Moran. He probably couldn't gain access to the horses, but he thought there was a chance he could get to that equipment in those carriages. He had a folding knife which was sharp as a razor. He knew if he could slice part way through those bridle reins or those saddle girths, he had a good chance of taking care of a rider in a race. Then, by god, he would be able to sleep through the night.

Johnny Moran knew enough about the racing game that it wasn't unheard of for some men to pad their bets by underhanded means. He fully intended to make sure that the Redbird was carefully watched over from now until race time. From then on his fate was in the hands of Jimmy Sykes. He had four dollars invested in the red colt with the hope of getting back twenty. What he didn't count on was not the horse being tampered with, but the tack.

While Maj. Thornton and his jockey were having supper, Miss Velma came over to visit their table. The major said, "We were thinking of coming to your church tomorrow, ma'am, would that be acceptable?"

"Oh my, Major, you'd be as welcome as the flowers in spring," she replied. "You all come on by in the morning and I'll feed you breakfast, and we'll walk over from here. Rev. Hardy would be delighted to have you there. Now, do we get to see what Jimmy gonna wear in the race tomorrow?"

The major said, "Sure, Jim, go put on your racing shirt so the folks can see it."

Jimmy ran to the back room and returned a few minutes later. The shirt was white silk, with red stripes an inch wide going vertically on the front and back. There was loud applause in the room. A number of people wanted to feel the shirt for themselves to make sure it was real silk. A colored boy in a flashy shirt and high boots was a sight to behold. The major made a mental note to get a photograph made before they returned home.

Late Saturday night there was a half moon. Dick Decatur had drunk a few glasses of beer, but his balance felt good. He stayed close to the buildings as he carefully crept around from the back of Shaughnessy's along a hard dirt alley to the corral in back of Moran's. Standing for a few minutes under the eaves of a building he made a careful study of two carriages that stood in the corral. One buggy was empty except for a carpetbag. There were two saddles and some other gear in the back of a buckboard, he figured the smaller of the two saddles was the one that would be in the race. He got down on to his hands and knees and crawled to the fence and stepped through. He rose and took three steps and he was next to the buckboard. He reached under the small saddle and grasped the girth strap and pulled it out. He turned the inside up in his left hand. He reached in his pocket for his folding knife. He opened it and held it in his right hand. Holding the girth strap in his palm he made a slice across it, trying to cut halfway through. Next he reached for one of the bridle reins. He made a cut into it about halfway from the bit to the end. He winced when he nicked the palm of his hand, but the deed was done. If the rein broke during the race the jockey would lose control. If the girth broke, the jockey would fall onto the track. There was no way on earth this horse was going to win the race. Now all he had to do was sneak back to the saloon. He felt like laughing but he stifled it. The joke would be on the jockey riding the red horse in the morning.

Chapter 21

Sunday was a beautiful. Jimmy was waiting in the dining room when the major arrived. There was hot biscuits and gravy, eggs and ham, and hot coffee. Jimmy was wearing his red-and-white silk shirt, so Velma tied a big napkin around his neck so it wouldn't get spilled on. The major was wearing his top hat and frock shirt, and looked very distinguished. Big Jim drank three cups of Velma's coffee. Jimmy had a cup with his biscuits and gravy.
He didn't feel much like eating, and they still would have time for dinner at noon before the race.

When they set off for Rev. Hardy's African Methodist Episcopal church, it was approaching ten AM. It felt a little strange to Maj. Thornton walking next to Little Jim and Miss Velma with an entourage
of Africans walking behind. It seemed like it was a march- signifying something, he wasn't sure what, but all the same, it was significant of something.

The singing was beautiful. He felt that these simple working-class people were holding nothing back in performing their hymns. The choir was in the front of the church instead of the back, and they swayed in time to the music. The congregation were unrestrained in adding their voices to the hymns. He recognized most of the hymns as being what he had thought of as 'Negro Spirituals'. That was actually just a white man's take on what were really just African people's hymns.

Preacher Hardy's sermon was on 'Family Ties; Corporal and Spiritual.' He did a thorough job of expounding on what family means, and on what corporal and spiritual mean. Big Jim came away feeling like he had been in a dream. These people had had their spirits lifted and they were all in a good mood. They may not have a lot, but they were thankful for every little blessing that was theirs. He felt like he understood them a little better.

Sunday dinner was like a huge celebration- more like Thanksgiving than just your average Sunday. But Big Jim was thinking too much about what was happening at two o'clock to have much of an appetite. He noticed that Little Jim wasn't eating much either. It was understandable. As soon as they could pull themselves away, they were on their way to Moran's to collect their horses. They saddled Redbird and Mockingbird so they could ride down to the Fairground. Moran was riding down as well- leaving Danny to keep an eye on the stable.

The major asked Johnny Moran, "How do they start these races? I haven't seen any kind of starting gate."

"Oh, they just hand start. Each horse has their own man holding until the start. Would you like me to hold for you?" Johnny asked.

"Ah, no, I'll do it, but thanks for the offer," said the major.

By the time they were headed for the track there was a sizable crowd walking, driving, and riding in that direction. Big Jim couldn't help but wonder if this big red colt was the fastest within ten miles of where they were. They would soon know.

There were a total of six structures in front of the track. Five of them were stables which could be hired out to owners of horses involved in the races. The other building was a long lean-to which offered some protection to spectators in inclement weather. All of these buildings were made of rough-cut lumber and weren't meant to be permanent. They were covered in simple white-wash. The roofs of the buildings could be accessed with ladders for any brave souls who wanted a better view of the races. At half-an-hour before race time, the roofs were becoming full.

It was easy to figure out who the jockeys were. They all wore brightly colored shirts. One wore blue and white, two wore yellow and white, one wore green and white. The other three wore red and white, but Jimmy wore the only red-and-white stripes.

Little Jim led Redbird to the water trough in case he was thirsty. The horse put his lips to the water and sucked in water for about ten seconds. He may have been a little thirsty, but not much. The boy knew that after the race he would be ready to drink more. Several times Jimmy was asked if his horse could run. He simply told them, "I don't know, purty soon we'll find out."

To Maj. Thornton it seemed that this crowd of people, which numbered more than two hundred, were, for the most part, unruly. Gambling was supposedly illegal, yet people were loudly making their offers to 'bet even money on number one' or whatever horse they picked to win. There were quite a few people wandering through the crowd encouraging others to eat or drink at a particular restaurant or saloon. One man was trying to sell a 'very nice bridle with a steel snaffle bit'.

There was a sign on the side of the largest building that read, "All entered horses report here." Big Jim reported there and was asked the name of his horse.

He answered 'Cardinal Archbishop', and he was supplied with two small white cloth flags with the number eight applied.

Maj. Thornton asked his jockey, "Do you have 'butterflies', Jim?"

He answered, "I guess I do."

"So do I," said the major.

Besides Bald Eagle there were six other horses. Some looked like legitimate thoroughbreds, some didn't. There was a tall black horse named Coal Man- he was number one. There was a dark chestnut named Gingerbread- number two. There was a smaller black named Count Pulaski- number three. There was a dun horse named Candy Man- number four. Number five was a brown filly named Chocolate Drop. Number six was a gray named Rain Cloud. Baldy was number seven. Just making a visual comparison, Maj. Thornton gave a chance of winning to only two others besides Redbird- Baldy and the brown filly. The purse was two hundred dollars out of a twenty-five dollar entry fee, so Big Jim was thankful for these optimistic horse owners.

As they approached the starting area only three horses displayed the skittishness associated with racehorses- the three Big Jim had picked. The filly was the hardest to keep under control. Something about this odd collection of people, well-dressed and shabbily-dressed, old and young, various races, different backgrounds, gave the major the impression of mass disorganization. He asked himself if it was even possible for there to be any kind of standardization or structure that was necessary to carry on a sporting event, or any event at all, in this place at this time in history. The gospel of Matthew went through his mind, "...But what did you go out to see? A reed shaken by the wind, a man dressed in soft garments?" Well, what did he expect? Now there was nothing to do but brace himself and see if he could accept the outcome.

He gave Little Jim a leg up into the saddle and helped him get his boot-toes into the stirrups. He handed him his quirt.

He knew Jimmy wouldn't use it, but it was part of the ensemble. Then he just held onto the bridle. Redbird stamped his feet a few times. The brown filly was dancing in circles. Of course they're born to run- in their drive as much as in their stature.

A man was standing at the side of the track with a white flag in his hand- the starter. All the holder's eyes were on him. He raised the flag. The seconds ticked by, Redbird was straining against the bit. The flag dropped and the horses were released. Clods of dirt and grains of sand filled the air. The horses bumped and jostled each other as they pounded their way into the first turn. Big Jim couldn't see which horse broke out first. Into the turn he couldn't make out who was ahead. All he could see was a mass of horses and jockeys trying to pull ahead. But coming out of the turn and into the back stretch, yes! Redbird was in the lead. He was ahead of the brown filly by half a length. He seemed to inch his way forward, hiding the filly as he went. Halfway down the stretch he was gaining, then Jimmy was leaning forward. What for? He was wobbling in the saddle, then he was over the colt's neck. Redbird was losing ground- what was happening? He was off his stride. "Oh, God," Jim thought, "I hope the boy doesn't fall." Jimmy was way up on Redbird's neck. Why? what was happening? They were going into the far turn and he saw the saddle slip, and twist, and fall away. The filly was ahead by a length. But suddenly it looked like Redbird was back into his stride. Big Jim ran toward the far turn, pushing his way through the crowd. He was yelling, "Hold on, Jimmy, hold on."Then he saw them rounding the turn and coming into the home stretch. The boy was still on the colt's back- "Thank God," he thought. He turned around and ran back toward the finish line.

Before he got there the race was over. Out of nowhere Johnny Moran was next to him. He yelled, "Johnny, run over and find the saddle- it's in the backstretch somewhere."

"I'll find it, Major," Moran yelled back.

The major ran toward the horses. His eyes scanned the horses and riders. Jimmy and Redbird were trotting towards him. "Jimmy, are you all right?" he gasped.

"I'm fine, Major," he said, "Somebody cut my cinch strap."

"I know, I know, how did you stay on?"

"I wrapped my arms around his neck and pulled my knees up on his shoulders. You tole me to hold on, no matter what, that's what I did. He couldn't run with that saddle back by his belly, so I kicked it with my right foot and it fell off."

"That was fine, Jimmy, you are amazing. Was he gaining, once the saddle was gone?"

"I don't know, sir, I was havin' such a hard time holdin' on I couldn't tell."

Moran arrived, carrying the saddle. "The girth's been cut, they tried to undermine you."

"I know," the major replied, "they couldn't stand up to the challenge so they scuttled us."

"Good day, Jim," someone said. He turned around, it was Col. Fordyce.

"Well, Sam, did you see what happened?" Major Thornton asked.

"I saw it, somebody tried to ruin you, but it didn't work," the Colonel replied.

"How do you mean?" Big Jim asked.

"For God's sake man, you won anyway," Sam proclaimed.

"We won, are you sure?" Big Jim blurted out.

"I was on top of a building, he was ahead by a neck, at least." Sam answered.

"Did you hear that Jimmy? We won," cried the major.

"Yeah, I heard, he did it on his own," Jimmy said.

Moran said, "No, you stayed on, you can't win if you fall off. You and that horse both did it."

Col. Fordyce said, "Let's retire to Col. Warren's place for the post-race." Together they walked over to the saloon. Moran volunteered to wait outside with Redbird As they entered, a man was announcing very loudly, "The rules require that the horse must be bridled and saddled and ridden by a jockey in the race."

Col. Warren rose to his feet, "The horses were all bridled and saddled and ridden in the race. The rules also say that horses not ridden by a jockey across the finish line will be disqualified. All the horses crossed the finish line ridden by jockeys. It does not say horses must be wearing saddles across the finish line. The winning horse is number eight, Cardinal Archbishop. The second place horse is number five, Chocolate Drop. The third place horse is number seven, Bald Eagle. All losing wagers must be paid out."

The room broke out in loud arguments as soon as Col. Warren finished speaking. He immediately began hammering on the bar with a mallet. "Hear, hear. Col. Sam

Fordyce wishes to speak, please listen. Anyone who doesn't listen will be removed from the building."

Col. Fordyce stood up on a chair and announced in a booming voice, "Ladies and gentlemen, Col. Warren has advised us on the rulings of this race and the rulings of this race shall stand. I have participated in horse racing in ten different states, including here in Arkansas. I have never before witnessed such a mean and cowardly display of sportsmanship as we have witnessed today. Some person or persons have practiced high skullduggery in a low and base attempt to bring injury and mayhem upon a competitor in this sporting contest. The Ethiopian jockey is to be highly commended for his display of skill and courage to ride his mount on to victory despite being faced with the utmost danger in finishing the race. It is my earnest hope that whosoever is involved in the criminal mischief we've seen today will be prosecuted for endangerment and attempted murder and barred from any involvement in racing in this state and in every state in the union. I congratulate Maj. Thornton, his Ethiopian jockey, his horse, Cardinal Archbishop, and every person who participated in his victory today in Hot Springs, Arkansas. Thank you all." The room broke into applause.

Jimmy pulled on the major's sleeve. "What did he say I was?"

Big Jim chuckled, "He called you an Ethiopian. Ethiopia is a very old country of black people in east Africa. Proud people with a rich history, like Egypt. He's just trying to show you some respect. He's proud of you, we all are, son. You made us all proud.

Outside Johnny Moran was holding Redbird. "Let's walk back to the stable," said Big Jim, "we can talk about it on the way."

"I must leave you, gentlemen," said Col. Fordyce, "congratulations to all of you."

"I can't thank you enough, Col. Fordyce," said Maj. Thornton, "Your support made all the difference."

"Think nothing of it, you know where to find me whenever you're in the area." the colonel said before he departed.

As they were walking back to the stable, Johnny said, "If I'm not mistaken, one of your reins has also been cut."

Maj. Thornton looked closely to the place Moran showed him. "Look here Jim, a second piece of treachery."

Jimmy looked at the rein. "You right, but you know, I don't ever use that part of the rein, I'm holdin' way up close to the bit."

When they got to Moran's place, Johnny said, "I'll tell ya how we're gonna find out about that back stabbin', it has gotta be one of these local boys that was in on it. Sooner or later they won't keep it a secret anymore. They'll be dyin' to tell somebody about it- even sooner if they was successful, but the word'll get out. 'Guess what I did to them West Creek folks...' then we'll know, it won't stay a secret forever."

"Well hopefully, in time," said Maj. Thornton, "there will be more organization in this whole area. We'll have better law enforcement around the track and all over the territory. This incident will bring it about as much as anything else."

"You're right about that Major, and Danny and I will keep our ears to the ground until we hear something," Moran said, "Speak of the devil, there he is." Danny was all smiles.

"I'm sorry I let this happen," Danny said, "I was keeping a close watch on the horses but I never thought about the tack."

"Neither did I," said Little Jim, "but now we know we got to do that, cuz somebody just snuck in here an' messed with that saddle."

The two Jims bid goodbye to John and Danny and walked over to Valley St. "Let's go up to the hotel," said Maj. Thornton, "I think there might be some people we shouldn't miss meeting with." As they came to Valley St. a hansom cab driven by a black man stopped and offered them a ride. "We're going to the Arlington," Big Jim told him.

"Yes, suh, just where I'm goin'," the cabby replied, Is this the young man that rode that 'Cardinal' horse in the race today?"

"Yes, sir," said Jimmy, "I'm Jim Sykes and this is my boss Maj. Jim Thornton."

"I'm Ken Davis, and I'm proud to meet both of y'all. Everybody in town knows about what happen in that race, an' we're all really proud of you, boy," the driver said.

"I was just holdin' on cuz I knew them horses would run over me if I fell off," Jimmy explained.

"Don't sell yourself short, Jim," said the major with a chuckle, "you're the man of the hour. Take a deep breath, I think you're going to be the topic of conversation for a while."

When they reached the hotel Big Jim tried to pay the driver. "Oh, no suh, this on me. I'm proud that y'all came by an' I got to carry y'all to the hotel. Wait 'til I tell all my friends." They thanked Mr. Davis and walked up the steps to the hotel.

Leon came down the steps, "Little Jim, I'm proud to see you, boy."

Maj. Thornton chuckled, "We're all proud of him. I thought we'd come in and see if folks would want to see us."

They do, they do," said Leon, "y'all just come on in."

The lobby of the hotel was occupied by about a dozen well-dressed people. Col. Fordyce was sitting in an upholstered chair with a high-ball glass in his hand. When he saw Maj. Thornton and Little Jim he rose and ushered them in. Maj. Thornton took a seat on a divan and a busboy brought over a small stool for Jimmy. Big Jim assumed that it was the 'correct' etiquette for 'colored help'. The colonel addressed the room, "I would like you meet Maj. Jim Thornton from West Creek, Arkansas, whose horse 'Cardinal Archbishop' won the first race of the season at the Fairground, and this is his Ethiopian jockey, Little Jim Sykes- whose resourcefulness saved the day when a treacherous trick was pulled on him." There was a round of applause and several people came forward to shake the major's hand. Some of them shook Little Jim's hand as well.

Col. Fordyce said, "Little Jim, would you accompany me to the kitchen, you can come too Major, there are some folks who would like to meet you." Together they walked through the dining room and into the kitchen. The colonel said, "Folks, I'd like you to meet Maj. Thornton and Little Jim Sykes- their horse 'Cardinal Archbishop' won the first race today, with Jimmy in the saddle."

All the men in the kitchen wanted to shake Jimmy's hand and all the women wanted to give him a hug. It was a little bit embarrassing but he suffered through it. Big Jim realized that there were a few people at Velma's who wanted to see the boy as well. So they made their farewells and headed down to the Smokehouse. The crowd there roared when they came in. The men picked Jimmy up and carried him around the room. He was still embarrassed, but he was getting used to the attention. The major accepted Velma's offer to feed them supper and they ate very well. It finally came time for Big Jim to go back to the hotel. He said goodbye and walked back toward Valley St. As he walked he kept thinking how uneven it seemed that a boy of a certain race couldn't accompany his employer in a public place. It was as though he and the boy were both caught between two worlds- closely connected but held apart by an invisible force.

Maj. Thornton slept well that night. He thought about the fact that he and his jockey would be returning home soon and his son wouldn't be there now. When he visited the main desk in the morning there was a message for him. A man named Gossage was challenging his horse to a match race

where the odds would be two-to-one and the winning margin would have to be 'daylight'- a length plus a few inches. He thought it over several minutes. Here was somebody who was so involved in gambling on horses, but didn't have a close match to work with, that wanted to create competitiveness by going to an extreme. He wasn't interested, and he left a message to that effect for the man at the desk. There being no pressing reason to stay any longer in Hot Springs, he checked out of the hotel. He carried his bag to the front steps of the hotel, where Leon came to meet him.

"Are you leaving us, sir?" Leon inquired.

"Yes, I believe so, I'm on my way down to pick up my employee."

"Well, let me get you a cab, sir." Leon waved to a driver in a carriage-for-hire and the major was soon on his way to Malvern Road. Once he arrived at Velma's smokehouse they bid farewell to Velma and her staff and walked over to Johnny Moran's. It wasn't long until they had the buckboard loaded and Redbird saddled. Moran had patched the cinch strap together with a scrap of top-grain leather. Maj. Thornton paid Moran five dollars and gave Danny a silver dollar. Moran said, "I'll get you some change."

The major said, "Don't bother, you've been a valuable asset to us and so has Danny. I'll be back in the future and I hope to be able to work with you again." They said their goodbyes and the major and Little Jim headed back south. They had made some memorable friendships on their way to Hot Springs and now they had a chance to visit some of those same people at a more leisurely place. Of course, they now had the opportunity to relate the story of Redbird's victory, the treacherous attempt to undermine the competition, and all the details of what happened while they were in Garland County.

Chapter 22

When they visited Henry Lichtenberg they got to stay with his family as they had before. Maj. Thornton asked about the possibility of the lumber camp becoming a town sometime in the future. The colonel told him that they had exactly that idea in mind and discussions had already begun on what name they would give their town. The name 'Marquand' had been suggested- it was the name of the president of the Iron Mountain railroad, but some thought it was too hard to spell. When they reached Camden a lot of people were happy to see them, especially since several people had placed bets on Redbird, and were happy to get their money.

Back in West Creek a controversy had started. A teacher had been hired for the children of the area. Her name was Paula Griffith, she was twenty-five years old. There was no schoolhouse, so classes were going to be held in the Methodist Church. The white children of the community would attend her classes five days a week. On Saturday and Sunday afternoon she would teach the colored children at the Abyssinian Baptist Church. A small number of white people objected. When the Judge heard about the controversy he scheduled a public hearing for the second Monday in June. He expected Maj. Thornton to be back in town by then.

The two Jims arrived back at Darley Hill at three in the afternoon. The staff were delighted to see them. The women were all hugging Jimmy like he was their long-lost brother. Chester unhitched Mockingbird while Jimmy unsaddled Redbird. Chester was happy to see the two horses back home safe and sound. Mr. Brooks was wearing a big smile. "Now y'all got to tell us all about what went on while you were gone."

"All in good time, Brooks, I need to have a rest before that, and I expect Jimmy could do the same,"
the major said.

"Are y'all hungry?" Mattie asked.

"Not right now, Mattie, let us have a little rest and we'll have supper at the usual time," Big Jim replied.

At supper, Maj. Thornton and Jimmy went through all the details of what happened in Hot Springs. Everyone agreed it was a thrilling story and one they wouldn't soon forget.

"I hate to bring up the idea of the money," Brooks began, "but all in all, how did you make out?"

The major said, "Well, besides the prize money, which was two hundred dollars, we bet a hundred and twenty-five dollars. The entry fee was twenty-five dollars, so that leaves a return of one hundred seventy-five. The money we bet was doubled, so another one hundred and twenty-five was made. So all the people who bet, which includes people in West Creek as well as in Camden, got back a dollar for every dollar they bet. In my particular case, I'm ahead by one hundred seventy-five plus a fifty dollar side bet, which comes to two hundred and twenty-five. But, when you consider all the money I've spent to get to this point, I'm not exactly getting rich."

Brooks, said, "I see what you mean. But I know everybody here is mighty proud of you, and Chester, and this boy here, and Redbird, I just can't tell you how proud we are."

"Thank you Brooks, it's nice to know we're appreciated," Big Jim replied.

"By the way, sir," said Mattie, "the judge wants to see you when you get a chance."

"Jimmy and I will go into town tomorrow," Big Jim replied, we can talk to him then."

The next afternoon they rode into town with Big Jim on Redbird and Little Jim on Dancer. They first went to see Ira. Ira was happy to get his winnings but he was interested in how the bronze horseshoes held out. "They did fine, Ira. We might need to think about getting some more of that bronze rod."

Wendell and Tyndall were happy- about their brother's success as well as their jobs. Ira had told them he just needed one helper, but the boys told him they would both work for the price of one. Ira realized that they were hard to break apart so he just told them it was fine if they wanted to do that.

They were awestruck over Jimmy's description of the race.

"Why don't you stay here, Jim, and visit- I'll walk over and talk to Judge Jacobs," the major told him.

The judge answered the door. "Come in Jim, I was expecting you. Sit down, I want to ask you about something."

"Any thing at all, Isaac," Maj. Thornton replied.

"While you were away I found an opportunity to hire a

teacher for our town. A young woman named Miss Griffith. She will be holding class in the Methodist Church for the time being. Now I had to give consideration to the colored children. She agreed to spend some time on Saturday and Sunday at the Abyssinian Baptist Church with those children. Now, I understand that some of your help are literate, is that so?"

"Yes, Anna and Chara have a rudimentary reading skill" the major said, "They learned at home from their mother. Since they came to work for me they have helped the rest of my staff to learn to read and write."

"Are they sisters?" the judge asked.

"Actually they're twins," the major answered.

"Oh, I see," said Judge Jacobs, "Aren't your Jimmy's brothers twins as well?"

"Yes, they are," said Big Jim.

"Well, I wondered if your two girls could help out with teaching the rest of the colored children," the judge explained.

"Certainly," Big Jim answered, "I've got a few books they can use. Why don't we get together at some point in time-with Miss Griffith, and whoever is involved and discuss the whole matter."

"Splendid," said the judge, "I have a town meeting planned for this Monday to discuss this whole matter with our neighbors, why don't you plan on coming."

"I'll be glad to said the major." He said goodbye to the judge and walked back to the livery stable. As he walked he couldn't help thinking how there were so many complications that were developing that he had never thought about when he had made his decision to move to this part of the country. But what Judge Jacobs had suggested made perfectly good sense- that his two housemaids had learned the fundamentals of reading and they could pass that along to the other colored children. When he reached the stable Jimmy's whole family was there-Miss Pearl, Ivory, and Essie Mary.

"Good afternoon, Major," said Pearl.

"Good afternoon all," the major replied, "since you are all here I'll tell you the news. Judge Jacobs told me that we have a new teacher in town, Miss Griffith. On Saturday, and on Sunday afternoon, she will teach at the Abyssinian Baptist Church. My two housemaids, Anna Lee and Chara Kee, will be helping her. How does that sound?"

Tyndall said, "I don't think Wendell and I have time for that, we got a lotta things to do."

Miss Pearl said, "Now boys, you're so young, the sooner you learn to read the better off you'll be. We'll have time for all the things we need to do, but this is too important to do while you have the chance."

Wendell said, "Couldn't just one of us go at at time and the other learn from him."

Jimmy said, "Now you know, whatever one of you is doin' the other one gonna be doin' too."

"Yeah, I guess you right. I guess we gonna learn to read no matter what." Tyndall replied.

"Just think, Tyndall," Jimmy said, "you see somethin' with writin' on it, you know what it says."

The major said, "Well, Jim, that's very well put. Now Judge Jacobs is going to call a town meeting where we're going to discuss all these issues. But we've got to be getting back, so tell your mama goodbye."

"One more thing before you go," Ira said, "Wendell and Tyndall found a big mess 'o' muscadines just across the river. We just waitin' for them to get ripe."

"Very good," said Maj. Thornton, "We'll look forward to that."

On their way home Jimmy asked Big Jim where the white children would be going to school. "Oh, yes, we never talked about that, did we," the major replied, "they'll be going to the Methodist Church Monday through Friday, Miss Griffith will teach them there. Rev. Davis will let us use the church for free. I know what you're thinking, why don't all the children just go there. Well, you and I know that's what we should do, but it's going to take some time before the people understand that. In the meantime, I just want all the children to get an education. Now you, and your brothers and sisters, and all the colored children can go to school, you want to don't you?"

"I sure do, and I like Anna and Chara- this is gonna be fun."

On Monday at the judge's public meeting only a handful of people showed up. Maj. Thornton, Miss Griffith, Rev. Davis, Rev. Moody, and a few other white folks of the town. The Judge announced, "Well, let's begin. As you may know, Miss Griffith is our new teacher. She's a college graduate and she's being paid to teach our children. Rev. Davis is allowing us to hold class for the white children in his church, and Rev. Moody is allowing us to use his church for the colored children. The classes in the Methodist Church will be held on most weekdays from Monday through Friday. On Saturday, and on Sunday afternoon Miss Griffith will teach the colored children at the Abyssinian Baptist Church, does anyone have a question?"

Mr. Beasley rose to his feet, "Your honor are we paying this teacher?"

"Of course we're paying her, you don't expect her to teach for free, do you?" Judge Jacobs replied.

"Well why does she have to teach the colored children?" asked Beasley.

"The law requires it, Mr. Beasley. If she doesn't do it we'd have to hire another teacher and we'd be paying two teachers instead of one," said the judge, "Besides that we're not having to pay for a building. Now do you think you could handle this business of education better than I can?"

"No, your honor, you can handle it fine," Beasley replied.

"Does anyone else have a question?" asked the judge.

Mr. Shoal stood up, "I know lots of folks who can't read and write and they get along okay, do all the children have to go to school?"

Judge Jacobs sighed, "Mr. Shoal, which church do you attend?"

"West Creek Baptist, your honor," Shoal replied.

The Judge said, "It's my understanding that, as a baptist, it's incumbent upon you to read the Bible, isn't that so."

"Well, yes, I guess it is." Shoal replied.

The judge continued, "Now Rev. Moody, does the Abyssinian Baptist Church have a policy as regards the Bible?"

Rev. Moody stood up, "Yes your honor, to be a preacher you have to be able to read, and we encourage everyone to learn to read, in order to become a good Christian, because a good Christian should be able to read the Bible."

"Thank you Rev. Moody," said Judge Jacobs, "Now Mr. Shoal, do you see why we are making an effort to teach *all* the children to read?"

"All right, I understand, but believe me, there's gonna be some that ain't gonna learn," Shoal replied.

Judge Jacobs said, "If there are no further questions, this

meeting is adjourned."

As the people exited the room Maj. Thornton and Miss Griffith stayed behind. Miss Griffith said, "Major, I'm looking forward to meeting Anna and Chara, how old are they?"

"They're sixteen, they're twins you know," the major replied, "you may have some difficulty getting them to do different tasks."

"Oh, I can deal with that," Paula said, "it's really a good thing that they are colored girls- history has shown that the other children will be quicker to learn from someone of their own race."

"That's interesting" said Big Jim, "I get the feeling that some of these people underestimate the ability of the colored children to learn."

Judge Jacobs said, "Well you see, they're uneducated and so are the colored folks. They are bothered by the thought that, if the colored folk get educated, they'll lose their superiority."

"You're probably right," said Maj. Thornton, "I wonder what their life would be like if they didn't have other people on whom to look down."

So West Creek had a school. It was five days a week for the white children and two days a week for the black children. It wasn't the best that could be hoped for, but it was heading in the right direction.

Nearly everyone liked Paula Griffith. She was the kind of person who could put aside all the concerns of the world and just interact with all the children she had to teach. Anna Lee and Chara Kee were lovely children and she would come to know them very well during the next few years.

Chapter 23

Maj. Thornton had a decision to make. He had four colts, and he needed to decide which ones he would keep and which ones he would sell. It made sense to keep half brothers or sisters of Redbird since there was hard evidence that he could win races. But, since this was an agrarian community in which they were living, horses were needed for other purposes, and being able to sell horses for those other purposes was the practical basis for raising horses. He had a nagging feeling that he didn't really want to part with any of them, but he knew he had to. Well, at least he could get input from Chester and Jimmy, that was a practical thing to do.

After that they could start thinking about what they would do for the racing season of the next year.

One element of deciding which foals to sell is the sex factor. Since a mare can only have one offspring in a year, and a stallion can have many, it makes sense to keep more female foals than males.

The weather was mostly fair all that spring and summer, and when the time came to pick the muscadines Ira and the the twins crossed the river with fruit baskets and tow sacks. The muscadines were big and plump. They filled two bushels with muscadines, and the tow sacks with another ten or fifteen pounds.

They made a careful plan to get all their berries back in one trip. Ira stood in the middle with each hand on a basket handle. Wendell and Tyndall each had bags tied across their shoulders and one hand on the either side of the baskets Ira was carrying. It took them nearly an hour to get back to the ferry landing. Matthew saw them coming and was waiting at the flat boat when they arrived. "How much wine will that make?" he wanted to know.

"Oh, maybe five or six gallons." Ira told him. "I'd sure like to know who owns that land."

"Wouldn't the judge be able to find out?" Matthew suggested.

"Yeah, I guess he could," Ira replied, "I'll have to remember to ask him. Now you boys know what you got to do."

"What do we got to do?" Wendell asked.

"Y'all got to both be helpin' me for the next few days. I got to squeeze all them muscadine an' get them started makin' so I need y'all ever day for a few days," Ira explained.

"Oh yeah," Tyndall said, "We'll be here as much as you need us, Mr. Ira."

"That's fine boys, this gonna be a good year for wine, and y'all found the muscadines." Ira concluded.

Wendell said, "Mr. Patterson says Jesus turned the water into wine at the marriage feast at the Cane Break."

"Nah, that's Cana," Tyndall corrected.

"That's right," Ira replied, "But we can't do it like Jesus, we got to work a little harder. But he did make it so we got the muscadines to do it with."

Maj Thornton sat down at breakfast and there was a letter from Col. Fordyce. While he sipped his coffee he perused the letter.

"Dear Maj. Thornton, would you do me the kindness of sending the address where your son, David, can be reached, and please send him the following proposal. I should like to order a quantity of rails from Europe and have them shipped to New Orleans. If David is willing, I would like to contract with him to transport them up the river by means of barges. I understand that there are available steam powered tow boats which can navigate the river. I need to have them brought to Bird Point Missouri.   I would pay all his expenses in addition to whatever his time and work amount to. Ask him to write me as soon as he gets this message. I expect that we will be able to communicate by telegraph in the future. Thank you for your help, Maj. Thornton.

Sincerely,
Col. Sam Fordyce"

On a fine summer morning David Thornton arrived at the Hartmann Co. office in New Orleans.

"Ah, David," said Mr. Hartmann, "You've received a letter from your father. It was addressed 'in care of' this office, I hope it has something to do with business. Why don't you open it and read it before we do anything else." Eli handed him the letter.

David looked closely at the address, 'Master David Thornton, in care of the Hartmann Co. New Orleans'. It was definitely his father's handwriting.

He opened it and began to read aloud, "Dear Son, I have received a letter from my friend Col. Sam Fordyce who sent it from the Bank of Missouri in St. Louis. He is currently working on a project to build a railroad from southeastern Missouri to the border of Texas in southwestern Arkansas. He wants to offer to Mr. Hartmann's company the contract for shipping his rails, which he is ordering from Europe to be shipped to New Orleans, to be transported up the Mississippi river to a place in Missouri known as Bird Point. I do not have any of the details about the shipment, only that the distance from Bird Point to Texarkana is approximately four hundred miles and the rails would weigh approximately twelve hundred and fifty tons. I have given Col. Fordyce your address and you should be hearing from him soon. I have a feeling Mr. Hartmann might be interested in his offer. As for myself, I hasten to let both of you know that Sam Fordyce is a very well educated and accomplished businessman of the highest moral standards. If he says he is going to build a railroad I do not question his ability to do it. Col. Fordyce served in the Ohio Cavalry while I served in Kentucky, so you would expect him to be of impeccable character. Give my regards to Mr. Hartmann, and please let me know how things turn out with respect to Col. Fordyce's offer.

Your loving father,

Maj. James D. Thornton"

Eli Hartmann was staring straight at David, as though his mind was preoccupied. He didn't say anything for several minutes. Finally he said, "David, that's the most remarkable thing I've ever heard, I'm sure you understand what all that means. My mind is spinning at the moment. Tell me what you're thinking."

David swallowed, then said, "I'm a little light-headed myself. But, I imagine it means finding barges and towboats with which to do the transporting."

Eli closed his eyes for a second and then opened them again. "Well, yes, of course, this is only a question of towboats and barges. If we can move one barge then we can move more- a lot more. All we must do is try to acquire as many vessels as we can. Oh my, twelve hundred tons of rail. David, we've got our work cut out for us. Where is Col. Fordyce now?"

"Well, my father said he was writing from the Bank of Missouri in St. Louis," David replied.

"Oh yes, let's write to him right away," Eli responded, "start a letter and I'll pour us a glass of sherry. Sign your name to it at this address."

David wrote, "We received information from Maj. James Thornton about your need for the shipping of rails from New Orleans to Bird Point, Missouri. We will accept your offer and await more details from you with regard to dates and tonnage to be shipped.

Sincerely,

David W. Thornton c/o

Eli Hartmann and Company

New Orleans, Louisiana"

Eli Hartmann took a sip of sherry as he looked over the letter. "It looks fine to me, put it in an envelope and send it off. David, you've just become a success in the shipping business, cheers."

David said, "Thank-you, I guess we need to start trying to get our hands on some good-sized barges, and they don't have to be anything special, there's nothing fragile about rails."

"Yes, just as long as they stay afloat," said Hartmann, "but with towboats, the bigger the better, since we'll be moving a lot of weight. Now we've got other projects going, and while we're moving other cargo we can be on the lookout for the biggest barges and towboats we can find."

David said, "I'll broach the subject at dinner tonight, the Bourgeoises are an old Creole family, I expect they might know some people in the river traffic trade."

"Ah, the family of the southern belle you met on the levee last month," Eli replied, "find out if they have any connections in that regard; is Camilla interested in business?"

"She likes horses. She got a certain look in her eye when I told her my father raises thoroughbreds. I've promised to take her to Arkansas when the opportunity presents itself," said David.

"Well, we seem to be headed in that direction, who knows what will transpire," said Eli, with a smile.

Chapter 24

Maj. Thornton had a bay filly that he was very keen about. She was a full sister to Redbird, which was enough evidence for him to have expectations of her running ability. He had named her Priscilla, but they called her Catbird. She was a two-year-old the first year Redbird raced in Hot Springs. Big Jim could see no reason not to have a plan for the next season with Redbird running in a stakes race or some other event, and Catbird running in a filly race or a main three-year-old race. He wanted to talk it over with Chester and Little Jim. At supper that evening he asked the two to walk down to the stable with him so they could talk. On their way down, Big Jim said, "Let's go look at the fillies."
Chester and Little Jim nodded their agreement. As they approached the fence, several of the fillies came towards them. Three of them stuck their heads over the top rail.
"Somebody's been making pets out of these animals," Big Jim said with a smile.

"They just like the attention," Chester responded. The one they called Catbird pulled her head back and nudged the other two of her sisters. She had what we know as a 'fast metabolism' but they referred to it as 'high spirited'. She was long-legged and long-backed with longer than average pasterns.

"So, what do you all think of Catbird?" the major asked.

Little Jim spoke, "Well she look like she can run and she act like she *want* to run."

"That's right," Chester agreed, "But she so light."

"I don't expect she weighs over eight hundred pounds," said Big Jim, "she gets enough to eat, but she burns it off because she's so high-spirited. Jimmy, have you been on her?"

"A couple of times; seem like she takes my weight pretty well."

"Let's put a saddle on her and ride her down to the oak tree and back; and we'll let Dancer run along with her and see how she acts," the major suggested.

Little Jim and Chester saddled the two horses and led them down to the big gate.

The major said, "Now you two mount up and I'll hold them. Well, I'll hold the filly, I need to use my stopwatch,

Chester, you just hold Dancer back. On your mark, set go."

The filly bolted ahead as if she knew she was supposed to outrun the gelding. She held her pace well after they had turned to come back, but she wasn't stretching a lead. Big Jim was waving one hand over his head, but the two horses didn't slow down until they were almost to the paddock area. They were both breathing heavily. While they were unsaddling Big Jim said, "She seems to have run herself out, boys. Her time is fairly good, but she's too winded. Let's plan on running her alongside other horses and let her get used to being paced."

"How far is it to the oak tree and back?" Chester wanted to know.

"About a mile, I timed her at a minute and forty-five seconds," Big Jim replied, "which is reasonably good. It's the hot blood in her. We'll keep timing her and see if she really wants to run."

When Wendell and Tyndall arrived at the livery stable, Ira was holding a note in his hand. "One of you boys read this to me," he said.

Tyndall said, "Let Wendell read it, he's a better reader."

"No I ain't, gimme that note," said Wendell. Ira handed him the note. "It say, Mr. Blacksmith, please see me the next chance you get. Judge Jacobs."

"All right, you boys make sure all these horses got enough hay and water, I'll go see what the judge want," said Ira.

The judge answered the door when Ira knocked.
"Ah, Ira, lets walk over to the hotel, we need to talk." They stepped onto the porch and sat down in two wooden chairs. The judge said, "I understand you've found a supply of possum grapes."

Naw, suh, they's muscadines, they bigger and, more like a re'glar grape. Possum grapes is little bitty," Ira replied.

"Well that's even better," the judge replied.

Clothilda appeared on the porch.

"Can I get you gentlemen anything?" she inquired.

"Bring us a cool glass of tea with sugar," Judge Jacobs requested. She left the porch.

"It was supposed to be secret, Judge," continued Ira.

"Well, you know how that is. That's partly why I wanted to talk to you. Now, one way or another you're going to make grape juice, right?"

"That's right, suh."

"Well, I've done some studying about this, and here's what I think you should do. You tell me if I get to something you can't deal with. Are you with me?" the judge continued.

"I'm listenin', go on," Ira replied.

"I am going to get you some quart bottles with corks- they should be here day after tomorrow. You don't need to pay me for them, just give me two quarts of the juice if this works out. You go ahead and squeeze your juice. Then put the juice in a big kettle- biggest one you can find, and heat it up until it steams. Now it won't ferment- won't turn to alcohol, won't turn sour either. Then you pour it off into clean bottles and cork it with clean corks. Do you follow me?" the judge asked.

Ira nodded, "I think I do. If anybody wants to know, all I got is muscadine juice. Whatever folks wants to do with it, that's up to them. Am I right?"

"That's exactly right, Ira, exactly right."

Clothilda returned with their tea. "I can see you folks is talkin' business, I'll just let you be," she commented.

"That's right, ma'am, and if anyone asks, just tell them we were talking about my horse, Cloudy, and bronze horseshoes," said the judge. Clothilda smiled and walked back into the hotel.

"Now there's just one more thing," the judge continued, "What is the location where these muscadines came from?" the judge asked.

Ira laughed, "See, them two boys of Miss Pearl's found the vines over across the river. They went down there with Mr. Patterson and then me and them boys brung them berries back."

"I see," Judge Jacobs said, "Well, don't say anything to anybody about this, I'll talk to Mr. Patterson and find the location. I'll find out who owns that land- it may be up for homestead, or it may not, but I'll acquire that piece of land. Then we'll be able to make lots of bottles of grape juice."

"An' as far as anybody knows, it's all just muscadine juice," Ira said with a chuckle.

The judge tilted his head back and smiled, "Ouachita Valley Wild Muscadine Juice."

A few days later Judge Jacobs and Ira arrived at the ferry. "Mornin' guv'nor, Mr. Ira, would you like to cross?" Matthew inquired.

"You and I will cross. Ira will stay here while we're gone," the judge replied, "Put my horse and one of yours on the boat, I need you to guide me. It will all become clear as we proceed."

Judge Jacobs led Cloudy onto the flatboat and then Matthew led his mare on after Cloudy. In a few minutes they were on the far bank. "Mr. Patterson I need to see the patch of ground that gave rise to the muscadines," the judge began.

"Aye, I might have guessed," Matthew responded, "I assume this is all in strict confidence."

"Ah, yes, but the Sykes twins need to be reminded of that, although I understand they made the initial discovery," Judge Jacobs replied.

"Yes, they did. The area is just a short way down here." said Matthew.

On the way Judge Jacobs explained about the bottles and the pasteurization of the juice. When they reached the wild vineyard, the judge stayed in the saddle while he looked over the area. He could tell that they were in a natural clearing, and that the treeless open area had allowed the vines to spread over a area of about two acres. There were still plenty of grapes that could be picked. Finally he said, "Matthew, have you ever thought about putting in a homestead claim?"

"I haven't, sir, but I'd be interested in looking into it." Matthew dismounted and picked a handful of ripe muscadines and handed a couple of them to the judge. "Just bite a hole in the skin and suck out the fruit," he instructed.

The judge followed the procedure and a moment later said, "Ah, they have a nice flavor, this project seems to get better all the time."

"I would agree," Matthew replied, "but I can't help feeling that I'm getting something for nothing."

"Well, what do we all get every day? Food that grows out of the ground, horses who do the heavy work for us and we feed them grass that grows out of the ground," said the judge, "we just reach out our hand and there it is. Which reminds me, have you got anything in which to carry back some grapes?"

Matthew had a cotton sack in his pocket and they filled it with several pounds before they turned back. When they arrived back at the ferry, the Sykes twins were there with

Ira. "Now you boys remember," Ira told them, "anybody want to know about them muskydines, we just makin' juice."

"Well, Ira, things are looking well, thanks to these boys" the judge said.

Ira said, "Yes suh, an' you know what, when you sent that note over to me, these boys read it to me."

"Well that's fine," Judge Jacobs replied, "Miss Griffith's work is paying off already; yes indeed that is just fine."

Chapter 25

About twice a week they let the bay filly, Catbird, run with a handful of the three and four-year-olds, including Redbird. They made sure to feed her a ration of corn every day in an effort to give her more bulk. When she was running along with Redbird she didn't seem to have any trouble keeping up with him. Big Jim was using his red colt as a yardstick. He was guessing that the stretch from the gate to the oak tree and back as being close to a mile. In fact, Chester had been referring to it as 'the major's mile.' Allowing for the change in direction around the tree, he thought Redbird could run it in about a minute and forty seconds.

The time was approaching that they would be traveling to Hot Springs for the racing season. As they gathered for dinner, Maj. Thornton sat at the table in the kitchen with the help. "In case you all are wondering," Big Jim began, "Jimmy and I are soon to be heading back to try our luck in Hot Springs again. We'll be leaving day after tomorrow, is there anything we need to talk about while we're still here?"

Mr. Brooks said, "Well, I know a lot of us want to put some money down on hopin' you all win."

"Yes, I know you do, and I hope we're successful as we were last year," said the major, "but it is well to remember that this whole enterprise is an up and down kind of thing. We assume we're going to come out ahead in the long run, but we won't always win."

"Well, I think I can speak for most of us," said Brooks, "that we're staying on the optimistic side."
They had a good laugh.

"Well, tell me, how do you all feel about the school so far?" the major wanted to know.

Chara Kee spoke up, "We've been workin' a lot with Little Jim's brothers, and they have learned a lot, an' Anna Lee and me, we have learned a lot by working with them."

Anna Lee added, "Essie Mary and Ivory are learnin' too, it's just they not so excited about it like those boys. Like they always tryin' to outdo each other. I guess my sister an' I are kinda the same way."

Big Jim said, "We've got the Bible to read, of course, but I've ordered some books by Charles Dickens and Mark Twain, as well as some others, so I hope everybody will have something to read."

Mattie said, "It just seems like life gets better if you can read."

"I think so too," Chester added, "by the way, how long will you all be gone?"

"About ten days," the major replied, "if everything goes as planned. We'll get on the train in Malvern and ride to Hot Springs from there. If you haven't heard, Col. Fordyce is building a railroad from St. Louis to Texas. My son David and his boss, Mr. Hartmann will be shipping the rails up the Mississippi from New Orleans."

"That's just grand," said Brooks, "Our David, helpin' build a railroad."

"Yes, it is grand. Well, tomorrow I'll ride into West Creek and have Ira put shoes on Redbird and Catbird," said Big Jim, "and the next day we'll head for Hot Springs."

At the blacksmith shop the next day, Maj. Thornton asked Ira how he was getting along since he started bottling grape juice.

"It's a good thing I got the twins workin' with me. They can take care of the horses when I gotta be doin' somethin' else. They getting' where they workin' like two boys instead of one boy an' a helper. But they ain't here now- can I get you to hold for me til one of them gets back?"

"Certainly," Big Jim replied, "and take your time, these horses have to go quite a ways before we tend to their feet again."

Ira was using bronze rod again to make the shoes. They had thought about using brass but it was deemed to be too soft for the purpose of horse-shoes.

"Major, I got a question, maybe you could answer," said Ira.

"I'll try," the major replied.

"The judge told me that if I heat up the juice before I puts it in bottles, it won't turn to wine. Why is that?"

Big Jim paused for a moment, "The juice turns to wine when the yeast turns the sugar into alcohol. The heat just kills the yeast, so the sugar doesn't turn into alcohol. The idea came from a frenchman named Pasteur, so they call it Pasteurizing."

"That makes sense," said Ira, "but where does the yeast come from?"

"The grapes have a wax coating on the skin and the yeast is

in that waxy layer," the major replied.

"You mean to say," said Ira, "the yeast is already there- makin' the juice turn to wine?"

"That's right."

"So God musta meant for us to drink wine," Ira mused.

"That's how it seems." Big Jim said with a smile.

"Hey, Big Jim," the Sykes twins had arrived, "want us to hold Redbird?"

"That would be fine, boys," he handed the lead rope to Tyndall, "Wendell, why don't you walk Catbird around for a spell, she's getting stir crazy."

Little Jim was making a list of things he wanted to get when he got to Hot Springs. A wooden comb for Chester, pencils to share with the others as well as paper, pieces of Arkansas stone for nail files and whetstones- he would think of other things later so he folded up the piece of paper and put it in his pocket.

By the next morning Big Jim and Little Jim were packing their bags for the trip. They had decided to forgo driving a buckboard and so everything they carried with them had to fit into four bags which would straddle the horses like saddlebags. The bay filly was doing a lot of pacing and foot stomping. She seemed to realize she was making her first trip beyond West Creek and was eager to get started. Jimmy had twenty-two dollars in bank notes stashed in his boots. They had the idea that if they got robbed the perpetrators wouldn't think to search the boy, and Big Jim was only carrying ten dollars. At last, all the goodbyes were said and they were off to Hot Springs National Park. Col. Fordyce had convinced the government in Washington to make it so the springs belonged to the people of the United States, which meant that nobody owned it. They could only lease a part of it and build a bathhouse on it.

When they reached the Sumacs, they noticed that there were houses which could be seen from the road and were on the west side of the river. By the time they had ridden five miles past the Sumacs a light rain had started. They stopped and pulled their oilskins out of their bags. The filly began to jump around, apparently she was spooky about the oilskin. "Hold her steady, Jim and I'll come up from behind and try to get it over you," the major suggested. They finally got it over horse and rider and she seemed to settle down a little. Getting the oilskin over himself and Redbird, the major finally said, "Okay, we'll stop in Camden, I hope this doesn't keep up."

In half an hour it became a steady drizzle, but didn't get any worse. By the time they reached Camden they were both a little wet and a chilled as well. As they rode up to the stable Mr. Nunn said, "Well, it's Maj. Thornton and Little Jim, are you staying the night?"

"Yes we are," the major replied.

"I know Redbird, but who is this purty filly?" Phillip asked.

"She's Redbird's sister, we call her Catbird," said Big Jim.

"I'll take good care of 'em, Major," said Mr. Nunn

The major said, "Well Jimmy, is it the hotel or Big Annie's place?"

"Well, we know Lunettie's a good cook, I'd rather stay there," Little Jim replied.

"I thought you'd say that," said Big Jim, "All right, let's go."

Big Annie answered the door, "C'mon in y'all, better get out of them wet clothes. What's y'all's name again?"

"Big Jim and Little Jim," said Maj. Thornton.

"Well, Little Jim, you go on in the kitchen and let Lunettie help you out of them wet clothes," Big Annie instructed, "Big Jim, you just go on up the stairs to that first room on the right. Once ya'll get some dry clothes on Lunettie will have us some supper on the table."

"Hey Miss Lunettie," said Little Jim.

Hoo, boy, come hug my neck," she replied. After the obligatory embrace she said, "You got some dry clothes to put on?"

"I got clothes in this bag," Jimmy replied, "This time we got two horses we takin' to Hot Springs. Redbird, like befo' an' a filly name Catbird. I'm gonna ride 'em both."

"Oooh, you be careful, they tried to get you killed last year. Lemme put them socks an' pants by the stove so they dry out," said Lunettie.

Big Annie appeared in the doorway with Big Jim's trousers and socks, "Lunettie, put these clothes by the stove, I got to see if anybody else comin' for supper."

There were no other guests for supper so they ate in the kitchen. There were slices of ham, red beans, rice, and buttermilk. It was good, but Jimmy was still looking forward to fried chicken at Velmas.

Annie asked the blessing, and at the end Lunettie said, "An' Lord, take care of these boys, amen."

The sky was clear in the morning. The lumber camp they stayed in before was bigger; timber cutting seemed to be happening all around. Since they were making good time they decided not to stop and see Col. Lichtenberg. They reached Arkadelphia in the early evening and went to look for a livery stable. As they rode down the main street a black man said, "Excuse me sir, are you looking for a place to board those horses?"

Maj. Thornton said, "Why, yes, I am."

"Just follow me, I'm Bill Barker," the man said. He turned down an alleyway and walked fifty feet to his stable.

Big Jim said, "I am Maj. Thornton and this is my hostler, Jimmy Sykes."

"I only had space for two more, you're lucky I saw you," he said as he held the horses so they could dismount.

"This town has grown since we last came through here," said the major, "Are you the owner?"

Bill was unsaddling the horses, "Yes, I came here from Alabama, as did many of the new people here. There was a town in Alabama called Arkadelphia and it just seemed to fit this location. You have some fine looking horses, Major, could this be the boy who rode to victory last year in Hot Springs?"

Jimmy spoke up, "Yes sir, I am. We hopin' to do it again this year."

"Well, I'm proud to meet you, Jimmy," he said, shaking Little Jim's hand. The major held out his hand, "And I'm proud to meet you too, Major, and what are these horses named?"

The major said, "This is Cardinal Archbishop, and the filly is Priscilla. We'll be back early in the morning, we hope to meet the train tomorrow that takes us to Hot Springs."

"I'll have them saddled and fed in the morning, Major, good luck to you both," said Bill.

Bright and early they arrived at Mr. Barker's stable. The horses were fed and saddled and ready to ride. They said goodbye to Bill and struck out for the train station. The train hadn't arrived and the major left Little Jim with the horses and entered the depot.

Big Jim spoke to the clerk behind the counter, "I am Maj. James Thornton from West Creek, and I'd like to hire the use of a boxcar; I sent a letter about two weeks ago to let you know I was coming."

"Good morning, my name is Briscoe, I'm the station agent. I received your letter, you're a friend of Col. Fordyce, I believe."

"Yes, I am," said the major.

"There is a boxcar available, you want to carry two horses, is that correct?" asked Briscoe.

"Yes, I do," said the major.

"Have these horses ever been in a boxcar?" Briscoe wanted to know.

"They have not, but my helper has shown an outstanding ability to persuade horses to do whatever he wants, I don't think we'll have any trouble," Big Jim told him.

"I'll show you the car," said Briscoe.

The two men walked toward the empty boxcar. Jimmy led the horses along with them.

"This is my horse-handler Jimmy Sykes," said the major.

"Do you have a tin bucket?," Jimmy asked Mr. Briscoe.

"Coming right up," said Briscoe. The side door on the boxcar was open and there was a wide ramp from the floor to the ground. When Briscoe returned with the bucket, Jimmy took some corn out of his pockets and put it in the bucket. He let each of the horses nibble on the corn. He handed the reins of both horses to Maj. Thornton and carried the bucket into the car. He returned to the major and took Catbird's reins and held out his hand for her to nibble a few kernels of corn. He slowly walked toward the boxcar door letting Catbird eat from his hand. When they came to the ramp she stopped and looked into the car. He stepped a few feet up the ramp and held some corn out to her again. She carefully put one foot on the ramp and paused. Jimmy patiently offered her more corn. Slowly she put one foot after another onto the ramp and crept forward until she was standing in the car, and he let her eat corn from the bucket. Softly he said, "Major, lead Redbird in here."

Big Jim led his big red horse to the ramp. Redbird paused and lowered his head to the edge of the ramp, then he slowly followed the major up the ramp until he was standing beside Catbird. He put his nose in the bucket and took a mouthful of corn. While the horses were eating they cautiously closed the boxcar door. There was an open window on the side of the car so it wasn't pitch black inside.

Mr. Briscoe looked at Big Jim, "That's a valuable boy you've got there, Major."

"Yes, he is. I'd have a hard time finding anybody to replace him," said Big Jim.

Jimmy had brought along five pounds of corn in one of his bags. Big Jim bought the bucket from Mr. Briscoe since it was a little easier putting the corn in there than dumping it on the floor, which had large cracks. It was a new experience for everyone- this riding in a rail car with two horses. They stuffed big armfuls of hay in through the window.

The process of coupling the car onto the train was a little tricky, but they held the horses steady and kept them calm and eventually they were headed for Hot Springs on the rails. Little Jim made the comment, "Two horses and me that never rode a train before."

The major replied, "I've ridden a train before, but never in a boxcar with horses." Jimmy started laughing, and soon the major was laughing too.

They 'whistle-stopped' a couple of times but in about two hours they were at the depot in Hot Springs. Jimmy asked, "Wasn't that Hot Spring County where we got on the train?"

Big Jim said, "Yes, it was."

"But this ain't Hot Spring County?"

"No, this is Garland County. You're probably wondering why," said the major, "All I can say is that sometimes people do funny things that confuse other people, for no particular reason other than just because they can."

Chapter 26

After unloading the horses and saddling up, their first stop was at Johnny Moran's. Johnny and Danny had moved to a new location closer to the fairground. He had room for six more horses. His business was prospering due to the number of people who were coming from all across the country to take the hot water cure.

"Greetings Maj. Thornton," Moran announced, "a lovely filly you've got there."

"She's my pride and joy, Redbird's little sister; her name is Priscilla, but we call her Catbird," the major responded.

"Danny, show Jimmy where to put these horses in those two box stalls. Let them drink and get them some hay and corn," Moran instructed.

Danny said to Little Jim, "The major seems to like to give them horses bird names."

"Oh, she flies just like a bird," Jimmy replied, "her feet barely touch the ground. She ain't been shod but just the last two weeks an' she kin outrun any horse around West Creek 'cept for Redbird."

After they'd fed the horses they walked back out to where Big Jim and Moran were talking. "So she can run, can she?" asked Johnny.

"We know she has speed, we don't know what her best distance is. We'll try her at ten furlongs and see how she does," said Big Jim. "Well I think my jockey is anxious to see his friends at the Smoke House, we'll be around later to see how they're doing."

As they walked onto the porch of the Smokehouse they heard a scream. Velma was happy to see Little Jim. "It's my babeee- come here and hug my neck!"

Jimmy was a little embarrassed but he didn't mind too much. They were a little late for dinnertime but there was fried chicken, okra, sweet taters and biscuits.

It tasted just as good as it had the first time. Walter produced a bottle of wine which had come from Swiss people in the Arkansas valley. He passed out glasses to everyone at the table, including Velma, and they drank a toast to another racing season in the Spa City.

Maj. Thornton left Little Jim to visit with his friends while he went to register at the Arlington Hotel. As he reached

Valley St. he hailed a hansom cab which drove him to the hotel. While he was registering he inquired about Col. Fordyce.

The desk clerk told him that the colonel had ridden a horse to St. Louis to start building a railroad across Arkansas. "We all know how long it takes most of us to get to Hot Springs."

"Yes, although I only have to ride here from South Arkansas, Col. Fordyce intends to bring the whole outside world to the Springs, and a stagecoach is much too slow for that. Serving in the cavalry prepared him well for traveling on horseback, for he's done a lot of that," opined Maj. Thornton.

The desk clerk nodded, "He certainly has."

The major left his bag in his room and went to the bar. He asked the bartender for a pint bottle of Kentucky bourbon. "You want the best or the second-best?" the bartender inquired.

"Make it the best. What label is it?" Big Jim asked.

"Wellers. It's a dollar, but you will like it, the colonel says it's the best," the man replied. Big Jim handed him a dollar and put the bottle in his coat pocket.

When Maj. Thornton returned to Velma's place, there was music going on. He quietly seated himself at a table. A man was playing a fiddle and several people were singing, and most of the people in the room were clapping their hands in time with the music. The song was, "Crossin' Jordan I need not fear, halleluiah. Crossin' Jordan I need not fear, halleluiah. Crossin' Jordan I need not fear, Jesus gonna be my engineer, when we get that true religion, halleloo." Big Jim couldn't help but notice that the volume of the singing got a little quieter when he entered the room. He knew why- he was the only white person on the premises.

Velma spoke up, "Good evening, Major, can I get you anything?"

"About a dozen glasses, please- and go on with the music, it's beautiful."

They struck up another tune, "I got shoes, you got shoes, all God's chilluns got shoes, when I go to heaven gonna put on my shoes and walk all over God's heaven, heaven, ev'ahbody talk about heaven ain't goin' there, heaven, heaven, ev'ahbody talk about heaven." This verse was followed by "I got a harp, you got a harp, and I got a gown- and so on for six more verses.

When Velma returned with the glasses, the major proceeded to pour the bourbon - dividing the liquor evenly among the glasses. When they got to the end of the song, Big Jim invited everyone to have a drink on him. A few declined, but most of them took a glass. The major rose and lifted his glass, "To this day, to the racing in Hot Springs, and to the company at Velma's." Everyone raised their glass and then sipped the whiskey. "Now then," Big Jim said, "Does anyone know, My Old Kentucky Home?"

The fiddler said, "I know the tune, if you sing it I'll play along."

The major said, "Very well, I'll try to sing it. Oh the sun shines bright on my old Kentucky Home, 'tis summer the darkies are gay, The corn tops ripe and the meadow's in the bloom, and the birds make music all the day. The young folks roll on the little cabin floor, all merry, all happy, all bright. By and by hard times come a knockin' at the door and my old Kentucky home, goodnight. Weep no more my lady, oh weep no more for me, for we'll sing one song for my old Kentucky home, my old Kentucky home far away. Now that's the only verse I know. Thank you folks for letting me reminisce." They sang several more songs and then it was time for supper. When supper was over the major bid everyone goodnight and walked back to the hotel.

As he walked back, Big Jim thought about his extended family back in West Creek. He knew that someday, who knew how long, things would be different, and it would be folks like he and Little Jim, leading their daily lives, that would be the soil from which the new growth would sprout.

Before turning in, Jimmy walked down to Moran's to check on the horses. Danny said, "Hey, Jim, how's things with the major?"

"He's gone up to the hotel for the night. He came to Velma's for supper an' sang songs with us before he ate. He brung a bottle 'o' whiskey with him and poured drinks for the house. How's my girl doin'?"

"She's fine, so is Redbird," Danny remarked, "the major sang with y'all?"

"Yeah, he sung Ol' Kentucky Home," said Jimmy.

Johnny Moran came walking in. "Little Jim, you should talk to Col. Warren when you get a chance. He told me he could find you some work here if you wanted to stay for a while."

"I'll have to talk to the major before I could do that," Jimmy replied.

"Well sure, you and him would have to talk to Col. Warren, but these folks know you are a good rider and horse handler and there could be some good money in it if you stayed on for a while," Moran explained.

Little Jim said, "It's good to know that, thanks for tellin' me. Well, I got to get back an' get some sleep. See y'all tomorrow."

Little Jim was glad to get back and lay down. The trip was hard and he was tired.

The filly, three and under race, was the first event at the fairground. The start was at one o'clock. The entry fee was ten dollars and the prize was fifty.

Maj. Thornton, his jockey and Danny Moran arrived at the track at one thirty. The clubhouse had been given a fresh coat of white paint, and a small grandstand, large enough to accommodate a hundred people, had been built. There were four fillies besides Catbird around the paddock. Danny had been instructed to keep an eye out for any suspicious activity. Since the previous year they hadn't experienced any tampering with tack, but there had been a horse that threw a shoe during a race under suspicious circumstances. There had also been horses who had won races in Kentucky who were raced under false names for the purpose of winning bets from unsuspecting bettors.

By twelve forty-five, three more fillies had arrived. Col. Warren approached from the clubhouse. He was making the rounds of the competitors, making sure they would start on time. "Good afternoon, Maj. Thornton, do you have any questions?" he asked.

"No sir, I don't think so," Big Jim replied.

"After the race I want to chat with you about something," said the colonel. Big Jim nodded.

One thing that looked suspicious was that a couple of the fillies looked to be at least four years old. Maj. Thornton asked Danny to hold Catbird, then found a seat towards the top of the grandstand. Danny helped Jimmy to mount and then led the filly out onto the track. The flag dropped and they broke. Catbird couldn't break to the lead because the horses on both sides leaned in on her. By two furlongs she was in fourth from the lead, but she had running room, and by the half mile she moved into third. She moved into second and held on all the way to the finish. She had placed.

Jimmy dismounted and led her to where Big Jim and Danny Moran were standing. Little Jim said, "I'm sorry Major, I didn't move her up fast enough."

"No, you did fine, they squeezed you so you couldn't get out," the major said.

"It's my fault," said Danny Moran, "I should have let her move back and forth and shove those other two out of the way, next time that's what I'll do."

Big Jim said, "That's the drawback to not having a starting gate. I'm going to talk to Col. Warren about this, there is just too much inappropriate activity."

When he spoke to Col. Warren, he found out that there had been a lot of complaints about unfair starts and that a proper starting gate was a big item on the agenda.

"You wanted to see me about my jockey, Colonel?" the major asked.

"Yes, I haven't got time right now, but I believe there are several trainers who would be interested in using him."

On their way back to the stable, Danny said, "I think for now we just have to be ready to jostle with the other mounts and get some breathing room that way, otherwise you lose position."

"I guess you're right Dan, if they're going to push, you have to push back. "said Big Jim, "The stakes race is in two days, we have to make sure Redbird doesn't get held back."

"If you'll let me hold him," said Moran, "he's got enough size, I'll make sure he's got running space when they drop the flag."

"How do you feel, Jimmy?" the major asked.

"I feel like I'm gonna win that stakes race." Little Jim allowed.

"That's the spirit!" said the major, "that's the winning attitude."

Chapter 27

Little Jim had no trouble sleeping that night at Velma's. He fully expected Redbird to rule the track in two days. They'd gotten cheated that day, but he fully expected the big sorrel four-year-old would not let himself be pushed around by the other horses. And Johnny Moran was fully aware of what they might try to do.

Jimmy was up early the day of the race. He got dressed and went to check on the horses before
he sat down to breakfast. Danny was still asleep when he arrived at the stable, so he went to Redbird's stall and patted him on the neck. He picked up each foot in the usual procedure of vetting a horse. Both hind feet were fine, but when he picked up the right forefoot, something didn't look right; the inside end of the shoe had been pulled slightly loose. A cold chill ran over Little Jim.
He set the foot back down. He was standing there looking at the foot when Danny appeared.

"What's wrong?" inquired Danny.

"He got a shoe loose, I think somebody done been messin' with us again," he replied.

Danny said, "I'll get me dad to come look at 'im."

When Moran arrived he picked up the foot in question, "Easy boy, what do we have here? Ah, he's overreached with his hind foot. Who shod him last?"

"Mr. Ira at home," Jimmy said, "what's overreach mean?"

"The end of the front shoe stuck out just a little too far and he caught it with the front of his right hind foot when he was running. It don't happen very often, just once in a great while. Ira hadn't shod very many racehorses I'll bet."

"Naw, I guess not," Jimmy said.

"We'll get us a farrier to come reset that shoe." said Moran, "Where's Maj. Thornton?"

Jimmy said, "He should be at the Smokehouse soon- here he comes now. Mornin' Major, Redbird got a foot problem."

"That's a fine how-do-you-do, what happened?" the major asked.

Moran said, "He's got 'n overreach, nicked his front shoe with his hind foot. We'll get a farrier to reset it."

"Very well," said Major Thornton, "find somebody to reset it and we'll get some breakfast in the meantime, come on

Jimmy, I've got to have some coffee."

Big Jim had a sinking feeling when they got to Velma's and ordered coffee and biscuits. "I never noticed anything wrong on the way down here, did you?" he asked Jimmy. "What am I saying? I was riding him. I didn't notice anything."

Little Jim said, "Maybe when he broke into a lope he just nicked it, and then, the nail was loose and it kep' workin' more loose."

"I think you're right, that must be just what happened," said the major.

They walked back to the stable and the farrier was already resetting the shoe. "Maj. Thornton, this is Mike Murphy," said Moran.

"Glad to meet you, Mike, have you got it fixed?"

"We'll have to see," said Murphy, tapping the last nail into place, "let me clinch these and we'll let him walk on it."

He set the foot back on the ground, and Jimmy took the lead rope and led him down the center aisle. "Walk him up and down a few times," the major said.

Everyone looked closely at Redbird's feet as he walked. "Aaah," said Moran, "do you see what I see?"

The major sighed, "Yes, he's favoring that foot, it's gotten sore from him walking on it. It'll probably be all right before long, but I'm not going let him run. We'll have to scratch him."

"Major," Jimmy said, "can you get the entry fee back?"

Big Jim said, "No, we can't."

"What we gonna do?" Jimmy asked.

"Only thing we can do, enter another horse," Big Jim replied.

"You mean Catbird can run in place of him?"

"That's what I mean, now let's check her feet and make sure she's got four good ones."

As race time approached there was a modest crowd at the fairground. The prize was sixty dollars. Big Jim tried to find anyone who wanted to bet against the filly for win, place, or show. There were a number of takers and he had a total seventeen dollars wagered. The distance was one mile, so they knew she had to break quickly.

The major said to Jimmy, "Remember, she took second before, so break as quick as you can, don't hold her back at all."

"I know, I'm gonna let her have her head an' go,"

Little Jim replied.

As they assembled at the starting line, Moran tried to get her as close to the inside as he could without getting crowded. There was only one horse between Catbird and the rail. Jimmy could tell she was all excited, she was dancing and pawing. Moran stood in front of her and let her move from side to side. He told Jimmy he would step toward the rail at the start and let her slide by. When the flag dropped there was nothing but open track in front of her. She immediately took the lead but there were two other horses only inches behind. Around the first curve they kept that position, but as they headed down the backstretch she pulled ahead by a neck. From that point on she never gave up the lead, she led the race wire-to-wire. Lots of folks wanted to shake the major's hand, and lots of them shook Little Jim's hand and slapped him on the back and said, "Good ridin' boy!"

On the way back to the stable Big Jim said, "Well, young man, I guess we'll go talk to Col. Warren and hear what he has to say."

"You think I should stay here for a while?" asked Jimmy.

"Oh, I think we need to look into it more before we think about that. It might be a good thing for you or it might not," said Big Jim.

"But supposin' it was good to do, would you want me to do it?"

"Jim, let's just say, if you get a fair deal, and you've got a good place to stay, and it's going to help you, and you want to do it, I'm in favor of you staying here." Big Jim explained, "You can earn your living here, do you see what I mean?"

Jimmy smiled, "Yes, sir, I think I do."

Big Jim borrowed a horse from Moran and rode up to the hotel. He asked Leon to hold his horse while he went into the barroom. "Just sell me a fifth of that Kentucky bourbon," he told the bartender.

"How did it go at the fairground?" the man wanted to know.

"Oh, pretty fair. Cardinal had a sore foot so we scratched him and Catbird ran in his place. She won." he said matter-of-factly.

"Tell you what, Major, if you bring me a photograph of those two animals and your jockey, so I can hang it on the wall, the bottle's free." the bartender said.

"You've got a deal," said the major. They shook hands. He walked out side and got his horse from Leon.

"How's my Jimmy doin'?" Leon wanted to know.

"Placed on the first day, won today," said the major, "I'd say he's doing fine."

When he got back to the stable, Big Jim asked if there were glasses available. Moran had four shot glasses so they drank a toast to the Catbird and Little Jim. "Now, Mr. Sykes, should we go pay Col. Warren a visit?" asked Big Jim.

"I'm right behind you," Jimmy replied.

Col. Warren asked them to step outside with him, perhaps to not make it obvious he was negotiating with a black jockey. "Colonel, let's bypass the formalities, since we are both named Jim, we go by 'Big Jim and Little Jim."

Col. Warren laughed, "All right, just call me Bill. What I wanted to tell you, I have a list of people who would be eager to pay for Little Jim to ride for them, it would all be right here at the fairground.
Does he have a place where he can stay?"

Jimmy said, "Yes, sir, I can stay with Velma and her folks, that's where I always stay when I'm in Hot Springs."

"Oh, Velma's Smokehouse?" said Col. Bill, "Well, if I can find you there, you would get paid a half-dollar to ride a race, and another half dollar if you show in a race. How does that sound?"

"It sounds all right to me, Major, what do you think?" asked Little Jim

"That sounds fine to me, if you're willing," said Big Jim. "Now Bill, can I depend on you to look out for Little Jim's welfare while he's here?"

"Absolutely," said Col. Bill, "I'll make sure he gets from Velma's place to here and back again, and all the time he's here, he's under my protection."

The major said, "Then it's a deal." They shook hands, then the major said, "Congratulations, Jim, you've got a new job. Now by the way Bill, who is the photographer I've seen here making pictures?"Col. Warren said "He's Bobby Harris. His studio is on Valley St."

"Fine, I'll look in on him tomorrow," said Big Jim.

Col. Warren said he would look in on Little Jim in one or two days. Jimmy told him that he could be found at Velma's or at Johnny Moran's stable. As Jimmy and Maj. Thornton were returning to the stable, all of a sudden the major stopped and shook his head. "By gosh, Jim, your mother has no idea that you'll be staying here. I completely lost track of that."

Little Jim said, "Major, I thought of that myself. I don't think she would make any bother about that.
We can write her a letter today and send it. You'll be back at Darley Hill right soon after she gets it. If there's some reason she wouldn't want we to stay here, I can come back, but I really don't think she will mind."

"All right, I can see your point. Let's write a letter today then send it out tomorrow; it will be there in two or three days. Let's go to the hotel."

They sat at a table in the hotel lobby with a piece of stationary and an envelope. At the top, the major wrote, "Dear Miss Pearl, the following message is from your son Jimmy. We are writing from the Arlington Hotel in Hot Springs."

Little Jim took the pen and printed, "Dear Momma, I hope you are well. I am fine and Maj. Thornton is fine too. I have been offered a job to stay in Hot Springs and work as a jockey for the next two or three months. I decided to take the job and stay here that long. If there is any reason that you need to get in touch with me, I will be staying at Miss Velma's place, who I told you about before.
My boss will be Col. William Warren at the fairground and either he, or Miss Velma, will know where to find me. Give my love to my sisters and brothers. Your loving son, Jimmy."

Maj. Thornton addressed the letter and handed it to the desk clerk to be sent out on the train to Malvern in the morning.

They were at Moran's stable right after breakfast.
The major told Johnny that they were going to get pictures made. "So, you want these beauties saddled, sur?"

Big Jim said, "If you'd like your picture on the wall of the barroom at the Arlington, I can arrange that."

"Ah that sounds sweet as the angels singing, I must say," said Moran, "I'll leave Danny in charge."

Mr. Harris set up his tripod with his eight by ten view camera facing west down Valley St. Johnny held Catbird and Big Jim held Redbird and Little Jim was in the saddle on Redbird. Because of the bright sunlight it was a fairly short exposure- less than a second. They returned the horses to the stable and were back at the studio in a little over an hour. Mr. Harris showed them the glass plate negative.

"It will make a beautiful print, sir, I guarantee it," said Bobby Harris.

"Make me four prints, please," said Big Jim.

"Would three dollars be an acceptable price?" Bobby asked.

"That's fine with me. I've already traded one copy for a fifth of fine Kentucky bourbon," said Big Jim.

There was one print for the Arlington, one for Velma, one for Johnny Moran, and one to take home. The inscription read: Maj. James Thornton of Darley Hill, Arkansas with Cardinal Archbishop(l), Priscilla(r) trainer Johnny Moran and Little Jim Sykes up.

Little Jim went to the railroad station to help load the two horses in the boxcar. It didn't take quite as long as it had on the way up. Redbird showed no sign that he was favoring his front foot. Big Jim knew that the unloading when they got to Malvern wasn't to be any problem. When both horses were loaded Maj. Thornton said goodbye to Jimmy and wished him luck. "I'll speak to your mother as soon as I get there. If, for some reason she wants you back in West Creek, I'll come back straight away and bring you home."

"Well, all right, but I hope she don't do that 'cause I really want to earn me some money," Little Jim replied.

The major said, "I know you do, be careful, son, I'll see you in a few months."

As the train pulled out Jimmy thought about how he was away from home for the first time without his boss who was such a kindly gentleman.

Chapter 28

When Maj. Thornton arrived in Malvern he saddled both of his mounts since it was much easier for a horse to travel wearing a saddle than for a man riding a horse to carry an extra saddle. Finally he was on his way, riding Redbird and leading Catbird on a long rope. The road from there down through southern Arkansas was becoming quite familiar to him. When he arrived back at Darley Hill he asked Chester to hitch Mockingbird to the buckboard and drive him into town. While Chester was doing that he carried his bag to the house and asked Brooks to tell the staff he had to run in to town right away. "Tell them that everything's fine but I have to speak to Miss Pearl about Jimmy taking a job in Hot Springs. I'll explain everything when I get back."

Mr. Brooks said, "Yes, sir I'll tell them."

Miss Pearl was fixing dinner and needed some water to cook the grits. The twins hadn't come home yet and neither had Essie Mary. She didn't know what had become of Ivory. She had gone to take Mr. Patterson's laundry to him... that was it, she had started visiting with the Irishman and wasn't able to pull herself away.

Maj. Thornton and Chester drove up to the house. She stepped outside. "Good evening Miss Pearl, did you get my letter?"

"Oh, yes, I did, it came today," she said.

"Oh good, I hoped it would get here before I did. I'm sorry I didn't get your permission before I let Little Jim take a position in Hot Springs," said the major.

"Oh, it's fine, I know they all have to leave home some day. I'm just happy you could help find him a way to make some money," said Pearl.

Big Jim stepped down from the buckboard with the photograph in his hand. "I wanted to show you this picture we made in Hot Springs, it shows myself and Johnny Moran and Little Jim in the saddle."

"Oh, that's wonderful," said Pearl.

"It will be on display at the Arlington Hotel, at Velma's Smokehouse, and at Johnny Moran's stable. Velma, and Mr. Moran, and Col. Warren are all very fond of Jimmy and will be looking out for his well being while he's there," said the major "I've got to be going, but I wanted you to know about your boy before I went home."

"Thank you so much and God bless you, Major," said Pearl White.

As Maj. Thornton drove away, Wendell and Tyndall were just coming home. "Would you boys fetch me a bucket of water? I don't know where Essie Mary is and I'm trying to make us some supper," Pearl told them.

As they were driving home, Maj. Thornton related to Chester the story of Redbird's dilemma with the loose horseshoe. "Apparently some horses can catch the back of a front horseshoe with their hind foot when they are running."

"I never knew that," Chester replied, "and I've been around horses all my life."

"I'll have to speak to Ira about it, I guess you can't leave any of the back part of the front shoe sticking out beyond the back of the hoof," said the major.

"I just love that picture of them horses with Jimmy in the saddle," added Chester, " it makes me want to go up there myself an' see all that you been talkin' about."

"Well Chester, we'll just have to do that, we'll have you go up to Hot Springs with us next year," said Big Jim.

Ivory returned from delivering the Irishman's laundry and Essie Mary was not far behind. Everything was back to normal at the Yellow House. Pearl decided not to question the girls about what had caused them to be delayed. She thought she'd just wait and let the story come out on its own. And it did come out, in a way. As they were clearing the table after supper, Ivory said, "Momma, could Mr. Patterson come over and have dinner with us sometime?"

"Do you know if he *wants* to have dinner with us?" Pearl inquired.

"Oh he does," Ivory replied.

Essie Mary said, "She done asked him already."

"I suppose you heard her ask him?" said Pearl.

"Well, I went by to see if she was still there, and I heard her ask him," said Essie Mary.

"I think it would be fine for Mr. Patterson to have dinner with us, but I'm curious about something," said Pearl.

"What's that Mama?" Ivory asked.

Pearl said, "I know that both of you are friends with the man, but which of you is closer friends with him?"

The girls looked at each other before saying anything, then Essie Mary said, "She's closer friends with him," as she nodded towards her sister.

Pearl didn't quite know what to think, she just hoped that her younger daughter would find a boy she didn't have to share her attentions with.

When Matthew came for dinner it was a fairly warm day and all the doors and windows were open in hopes that a cool breeze off of the river would find its way through the house. They were having hominy grits and mustard greens with ham hocks. Matthew was filling Pearl in on recent developments in his life. "Well, it seems the land where the muscadines are located- where Wendell and Tyndall found the muscadines, that land is open for homesteading. I can claim three hundred twenty acres, which is what I put in a claim for. I'm going to build a house over there. I don't know what I'll grow, but there must be a lot of things would grow. I'd cut just enough trees to have lumber for the house, and with the muscadine juice and the ferry business, it just looks like things might go well. Ivory and me, we seem to get along real well. So, what do you think Miss Pearl, will you be my mother-in-law?"

Pearl couldn't help laughing. She dabbed at her eyes with her napkin. "Mr. Patterson, I assume you asked her to marry you."

"Of course he did Mama, we been through all that."

"Matthew, you got a way with words," Pearl said, "yes, I would be pleased to be your mother-in-law."

Chapter 29

Helen Baxter stopped in at the drug store. It had been eight weeks since she had talked to Ben Tilton about her lucky stone. Ben said, "Ah, Miss Baxter, I have news for you, and it's pretty good news. The people I wrote to in St. Louis want to send a messenger down here to see it. They are reasonably sure it's a real diamond, and if it's gem quality and is over one hundred carats, it would be worth about ten thousand to them, and they would exchange that much cash for it. Should I tell them to send the man down?"

Helen didn't speak for a minute or two, then she said, "I suppose you should. Do you know if that is a fair offer?"

"Well, they would have to cut it, and use it to make several pieces of jewelry, which would be quite expensive jewelry," Ben told her.

"Well, all right, tell them to send the man down. Thank you Ben, I'll of course share with you because you arranged it for me. What I've been thinking about, is that the negro children here are only going to school two days a week while the white children go five. I'm going to ask the judge if I could help to hire another teacher so those children can have more schooling. After all, it was a slave who brought that stone from Africa."

"I think that's a fine thing to do, Helen. I'm sure the judge would be most willing to help you with that."

Judge Jacobs arose at about eight o'clock on a Tuesday morning. He said to Mrs. Jacobs, "Mildred, I'm going over to have coffee at the hotel and speak with some people about the school, I should be back in an hour." It was only one person he was going to talk to, but he had a feeling it would involve more than just one. He walked into the dining room. Only Mr. Tate was there. He said, "Good morning, Seth."

Clothilda appeared from the kitchen. "Good morning your honor, would you like some coffee?"

"Yes ma'am, and a few biscuits," he replied.

Mr. Tate said, "Thank you for coming." The judge nodded. When Clothilda returned with the biscuits and the coffee Mr. Tate said, "Please sit down Clothilda, I asked you all here to talk about an idea that Clothilda brought up. Now, your honor, you have said there might be money available to hire a colored teacher for West Creek."

"Yes, I did say that," said the judge, "Please go on."

"I asked Clothilda about her acquaintances in New Orleans," Mr. Tate continued.

Clothilda said, "There is a young woman who is a friend of the family, who has graduated from college who plans on teaching. I will see if she would be interested in coming to Arkansas. Her name is Ornithine Fuqua, and she comes from a very good Creole family. Now let me add, that since teachers only work part of the year, she might work with me at this hotel the other part of the year."

"And if this all works out," said Mr. Tate, "I could escort her to West Creek when I am traveling from New Orleans."

"This all sounds very interesting," said Judge Jacobs, "Clothilda, why don't you contact her, find out what she would be earning in Louisiana and we'll offer her that amount or possibly more."

Clothilda said, "I'll let you know right away as soon as I can."

"Thank you, Miss Clothilda," said Judge Jacobs, "and thank you Mr. Tate, for the help you've both given me. Between us we've found a way for the colored children to learn to read."

Mr. Tate said, "This source of funding, Judge, can you tell us anything more about that?"

"Well, I can only say that it's a donation from a private party who wants to stay anonymous."

Clothilda said, "Well, we can ask God to bless this party anyway." The judge and Seth Tate both agreed.

A few weeks later, on a Sunday afternoon, a man on horseback approached the ferry from the east side of the river. Matthew assumed he wanted to cross so he pulled the flatboat across. The man's name was Charles. Matthew charged him a nickel. "Do you know where I can find Chester, I believe he works for a man named Maj. Thornton?" he asked.

"Sure, just head straight through town and keep heading west, you'll see the road on the left, it will take you there. Where are you from?"

"From Hamburg, I'm hoping to find some friendly folks who want to homestead," said Charles.

Matthew said, "I'm doing the same thing myself, we have a friendly judge here to help with that."

"That's good to know. I came here because Chester said

something about homesteading and it sounds better all the time," said Charles.

"Now, if you're ever in need of a place to sleep, I stay in this tent over here and I've always got room," said Matthew.

Charles said, "I don't know what to say, are all the folks here like this?"

"In answer to that question, no, they aren't. Some are downright hard to deal with, so the rest of us have to stick together, see," Matthew replied, "But go on over there and talk to Chester, then we'll see each other later."

As he climbed on his horse Charles was not sure if he was awake or dreaming, but he waved to Matthew and headed for Darley Hill.

With the location of the muscadines, and Matthew Patterson's homestead, there began a trend for friends of Miss Pearl's family to move to the area on the east bank of the river. This kept the ferry busy. It also created an area that was predominately African-American so that they felt safer there.

The next time Ivory came over to visit Matthew she came without Essie Mary. "I want to give you something," he told her, "I've had this silver shamrock since I was twelve years old. Let's say it's a symbol of our engagement."

"Oh Matthew, that's so sweet of you," she said as they kissed and held each other in an embrace that lasted several minutes."

They thought of having the ceremony in Brother Davis' church, but they decided to have it in the Abyssinian Baptist Church since most of the attendees would be black and anyone else would be welcome. Major Thornton and his whole household were there- they were all very fond of Little Jim's family.

The community on the east bank of the Ouachita came to be called 'Sykesville' in honor of the three brothers who contributed to its beginning. It thrived right along with West Creek, with small farms and houses and the sizable vineyard which expanded over the years and became a cottage industry.

Chapter 30

In the summertime, a few years later, Jimmy was in Hot
Springs in the middle of the racing season. More and more
there were white jockeys riding in the races. Because of his
skill and experience he was able to get into enough races to
keep him busy, but there were fewer and fewer young black
jockeys able to get into the business. He had hoped that his
younger brothers could become jockeys, but it looked as
though that would never happen. There were a lot of young
white boys that wanted to get into the business and they
were the ones getting hired.

 One evening as he was coming back to Velma's they told
him there was a telegram for him.
The message was simple, "The major is sick in bed, can you
come home?" It sounded bad. When he talked to Velma she
said, "You better go, it may be the last time you see him."

He felt like crying, but he held back the tears, "Yes, I think I
better," he said. The next morning he packed his bag and
walked over to Moran's. Velma had put some fried chicken
and biscuits in a bag to take with him. He had a a horse that
belonged to the major, named Sparrow. He told John and
Danny that his boss must be really sick because they wanted
him to come right away. As soon as he had Sparrow saddled
he headed out of town towards Malvern. Every now and
then he stopped just long enough for Sparrow to graze for
awhile so he wouldn't grow hungry. If the horse saw a patch
of tall grass he let Jimmy know he wanted to stop.

When they got to the Sumacs they were both very tired. It
wasn't long before he saw Chester coming his way. "You
didn't come a minute too soon," Chester said, "He won't last
very long."

When he got to Big Jim's bed, the man was racked with
fever, and everyone else was in a somber mood. "Major, it's
Little Jim," they told him.

He opened his eyes, but he didn't say anything. "He can't
hardly talk," said Mr. Brooks. The major squeezed his hand
and smiled.

"You the best man I ever knew," said Jimmy.

It was a sad thing that David Thornton didn't make it there
in time. By the time he and Camilla arrived, his father was
gone.

Maj. Thornton was well loved by most of the people in the surrounding area. The funeral was held at Darley Hill. Nearly everyone in the community was there. Everyone that wanted to speak had a chance to. And that was nearly everyone there. It was an unusual gathering for its place and time. People who didn't know each other became acquainted. White people who didn't know any black people by name, learned their names. They all came away knowing they had more friends than they'd realized.

Ivory found Jimmy talking to David Thornton and his wife Camilla. "Jimmy, I got to talk to you," she said.

"Excuse me folks, I got to talk to my sister," he said.

"Are you goin' back to Hot Springs after this?"

"Yeah, I got to, I might ride ten mo' races this year."

"I want you to take this silver cloverleaf. Matthew give it to me befo' we got married, but I got a ring now, so I want you to have it," Ivory said, "it's got a blessin' on it from a preacher man, for an angel to watch over you."

"Thanks," said Little Jim, "I need all the blessin' I can get."

After the funeral, Miss Pearl's family all went over to see Ivory and Matthew's cabin across the river. There were three cabins there, by then. One was Chester's and the other belonged to his friend Charles who had moved there from Hamburg.

"You built this cabin yourself, Matthew?" Little Jim wanted to know.

"Oh, I had some help from your brothers, and a few others from time to time. I did most of the work myself, but I can always find somebody to help when I need it," Matthew replied.

Little Jim said, "It looks like just about anybody could have they own place around here, don't it. What about you, Essie Mary, what you been doin'?"

Wendell said, "Her and Charles been spendin' lots 'o' time down here."

"Now, Wendell, I can talk as good as you. Charles an' me has been makin' some plans, just like everybody else."

Miss Pearl said, "You know, as long as Little Jim here, an' you an' Charles got plans..."

"But Momma, the man s'pose to do the askin'."

"Well, he's invited for supper, is that waitin' long enough?" Pearl asked, "Let's don't hurt nobody's feelin's." By then everyone was laughing, including Essie Mary. Wendell and

Tyndall decided they needed to go check on a trotline, and would be back in a short time. But they didn't go towards the river when they left.

Charles arrived in half an hour, and the twins were close behind. They were all smiling.

"Oh my," said Pearl, "Those boys lookin' like the cat that got the cream, are they goin' tell us what they smilin' about?"

Charles looked around at the people in the Yellow House. "All right, it ain't no secret. I just come from talkin' to Brother Moody. Essie Mary, I got to ask you somethin'."

"Are you askin' me to marry you?"

"Yes, I am." said Charles.

"I will marry you if it's all right with my Mama."

"It's all right with me," said Pearl.

"Then we gettin' married at the Church, day after tomorrow," said Charles.

The room broke into applause. When the applause subsided, Tyndall said, "Can we eat now?"

On the appointed day, at the Abyssinian Baptist Church, the whole African community was there. Mitchell Hendricks and Matthew Patterson were the only white men there. There was one white woman there- Helen Baxter. She was holding a small parcel under her arm. Helen came over to where Matthew and Ivory was standing. She said, "Mr. Patterson, which one is the bride?"

"That would be my sister-in-law. This is my wife, Ivory, she'll take you to her."

Helen followed Ivory to the south side of the church, where Essie Mary was trying get a straw hat to stay onto her abundant hair. Helen said, "Essie, I'm Helen Baxter, I have this extra pair of shoes which I want to give you. I think a bride should have her own shoes."

"Oh, thank you ma'am. Are you coming to the wedding?"

"If I'm welcome," said Helen.

"You *are* welcome, you can sit up in front with my sister and brother-in-law," said Essie Mary. She sat on a nearby log and put the shoes on and laced them up. They had fresh wax on them and they looked lovely. She looked up and Helen was gone; she hoped she'd see her in church.

Many people had brought food. There were biscuits, greens, hominy, and water melons. Miss Pearl had baked three cakes. She wanted to make sure that everyone got to eat cake on the day her younger daughter got married. There were also two and a half gallons of grape juice which had been sitting at the bottom of the well all night so it was nice and cool. There was a lot of singing and a lot of clapping. There was dancing, because the Hebrews danced when the Lord looked with favor upon them. The cake was wonderful. The wine was colorful. When all the cake was eaten and all the grape juice was drunk, it was getting dark, so everyone went home. Essie Mary and Charles had already left by then.

Little Jim was up early the next day. He didn't have a lot to carry with him. He went to say goodbye to his mother. Before he woke her up he slipped five dollars into her sewing basket. She would be sure to find it later and she wouldn't have a chance to tell him she wouldn't take it. An hour or so later she said: "Now that we can can write to you, where do we send it to?"

"Just put 'Velma's Smokehouse' Malvern Ave. Hot Springs, Arkansas. I'll be sure to get it."

His brothers were up and the three of them had some rice and milk for breakfast. "What plans do you all have?" Little Jim inquired.

Tyndall said, "We just gonna keep workin' for Mr. Ira. But we might get to work for Mr. David."

"I don't know if Mr. David likes horses like Maj. Thornton did," Jimmy replied.

Wendell said, "No, but Miss Camilla maybe likes horses better."

"Well, we'll just have to wait and see," said Little Jim.

Sparrow was at the stable so the three of them walked over. Ira said, "Well, Jimmy you leavin' again."

"Yes, suh, how do my horse's shoes look?"

"They fine, he's got hard black feet, them shoes will last a good while."

He mounted up and waved goodbye and rode west through town. He had gotten there to bury the major, saw his second sister get married and got to visit with his old friends, now he was off again to ride horses. But his future wasn't as sure as he once thought it was. But he felt like he had a home to come back to if it came to that. As he rode past the Sumacs he noticed there were three or four more houses in the community that he hadn't noticed on his way down.

Chapter 31

He was in no particular hurry to get back to Hot Springs. Whenever he saw a good stand of grass by the roadside he stopped and let Sparrow graze for a while. That way he got plenty to eat without having to spend money, and he stayed rested. There were people he knew between West Creek and Hot Springs, so he felt at ease making the trip even though he didn't have Maj. Thornton beside him. But he couldn't help but wonder how it might be different traveling through a predominately white area on his own. Even on the road that he was familiar with he felt a little uneasy being this far away from a group of people he knew he could trust.

When he was ten miles south of Hot Springs he felt a lot easier. He started thinking of the folks at Velma's, especially two girls named Linda and Jomeka, who worked in the kitchen and cleaned the dining room. There was a wide grassy area along the Caddo river where he took the opportunity to let Sparrow graze and rest for a little while. After that he mounted up and rode on into the town. It was early afternoon and he was hoping Velma had some leftovers he could have since he hadn't eaten since breakfast. He left Sparrow at Moran's and walked over to the Smokehouse.

Jimmy walked in the back door and into the kitchen. When Velma saw him she put her arms around his neck and said, "I'm so sorry about you losin' your boss and your friend. I don't think I met a nicer man in all my life."

Jimmy said, "Yes he was, we all gonna miss that man."

"Well how is your family?" Velma asked.

He told her all about how his sister had married an Irishman and he showed her the silver medal Ivory had given him. He told her about his other sister's wedding at the church. Linda and Jomeka appeared and were glad to see him. He spent the next several hours telling all his friends about the funeral, the wedding, and all about the folks in West Creek that had used the homestead act to claim their own land and build cabins. He was tired from his trip and he finally got a chance to lie down and get some sleep.

In the morning he went to call on Col. Warren.

"Little Jim, nice to see you," said the colonel, "So sorry to hear about your boss. I don't have anything definite for you.

If you can get down here early Saturday morning, I'm sure there'll be some folks needing a good jockey. A couple of races at least."

He thanked Col. Warren and walked back up to Moran's. Johnny was off at the tavern. Danny told him that there were a couple of horses they were boarding that needed to get ridden for exercise and he could make two bits a day if he wanted get in on it. He said he would like to do that. He told Danny that his two sisters had gotten married and showed him the silver medal. "She married a Irishman and this was his lucky charm. Then she got a ring and she gave this to me." Danny allowed that she must be a smart woman to marry an Irishman. John Moran arrived and Danny said, "Pa, Little Jim's got an Irishman for a brother-in-law."

"The hell you say," said Moran, "She's a smart woman to marry an Irishman."

In the first race that ran on Saturday, Little Jim rode a big roan gelding that outweighed all the other horses by at least twenty pounds. It was a mile race. The horse in the pole position jumped out to a good start. Little Jim tried to move to the inside but another horse tried to push him away. Because of the roan's size he couldn't be pushed, so the jockey swung at Jimmy with his quirt. It hit him on the side of his face, but he didn't pull back or lose position. Because of the jostling between these two horses it gave another horse the opportunity to get in behind the leader and the roan horse came in third. As soon as the race was over Little Jim ran to tell Col. Warren what happened.

"Thanks for telling me Jim, but the stewards didn't see it," said the colonel, "We'll keep an eye on that jockey, and if it happens again we'll bar him from the track."

Little Jim rode in another race later that day, but didn't show. The horse was so slow that he couldn't have done any better no matter who had ridden him. Jimmy walked back to Moran's feeling a little disappointed in the results of the day.

"How many did you ride today?" Moran wanted to know.

"I rode two, one showed, the other one didn't," he replied. "I got fouled in that first race. That jockey swung his whip at me- coulda put my eye out- but Col. Warren said nobody saw it but me."

"Yeah, poor sportsmanship, we see that every day now," said Johnny, "it's a rough business. Everybody wants to win so bad, they'd rather cheat than lose."

"It just seems like I'm not getting many rides anymore," Little Jim sighed.

Moran said, "I think the older colored jockeys are retiring and the new ones are mostly white boys. They're after the attention- want to see their names in the paper. That's why they're doing it."

"I'm just trying to make a living," said Jimmy.

"'Course you are, Danny and I are too, it's just getting tougher all the time," said Moran.

Linda and Jomeka were sitting with Little Jim while he was eating supper. Linda said, "Are you gonna stay down here for the rest of the summer?" Little Jim.

"I guess so," he replied, "They don't need me down home, I might as well just stay here where I got friends."

"You got almost famous when you first come here, didn't you?" Jomeka asked.

"Yeah, but 'almost' don't pay nothin'," Jimmy replied, "I just wish I could take care of horses all the time, if they would just let me do that."

Little Jim spent the rest of the season riding in races when he got the chance, or helping Danny exercise the horses that Moran was boarding.

One morning in October, Danny came to the Smokehouse looking for him. "Jimmy, there's a man at the stable, Pa wants you to talk to," he said, "his name's 'Prothro'."

Mr. Prothro was a tall dark-haired man. He held out his hand to Little Jim. They shook hands and the man said, "I'm Thomas Prothro. I came here from Wales when I heard there was cinnabar in the mountains west of here. I have a couple of horses which I'll use for the hauling. I understand you're good with horses."

"Yes, sir, I am. Been doin' that for a long time. What's cinnabar?"

"'Tis the ore from which we get mercury. Mercury is a liquid metal and it's valuable. If you'll come work for me I'll pay you twenty-five cents a day and your board, if you decide to stay. If you don't want to stay, you can always come back here."

"What kinda people lives over there?" Jimmy wanted to know.

"'Tis mostly deserted. 'Tis too rocky for farming, so few people have come there. If 'tis your safety you're concerned about, have no fear, I'll be close by at all times and I can handle any situation that might arise."

Jimmy said, "Well, I guess I'll go with you and see what it's like. I have my own horse, sir, can I take him along?"

"Splendid, of course you can bring him, the more horses the less work they'll have to do," Prothro replied.

Mr. Prothro had a big white mare and a heavy-set bay gelding which was a draft breed of some kind. Sparrow was bred to travel faster than either of Prothro's horses. Jimmy would have to learn how to 'pack' these animals for transport purposes. They would be carrying with them lots of tools and lots of food. Prothro asked Little Jim what kind of provisions they needed to take for the horses. Jimmy told him that corn was readily available and if they could find any oats, they were very good for horses. "Mr. Prothro," said Jimmy, "have you been to the place we're goin' to?"

"Yes, I have, but 'tis in a very secluded place, I can't take us straight there," Prothro replied, "we first find the Little Missouri river, then we follow it uphill and after some distance we'll reach the place where its banks are steep and narrow. That narrows is our destination."

Chapter 32

It was in the month of April, late at night, that someone set fire to the ABC church. Before anyone noticed the fire, the church was halfway gone, and despite the efforts of the neighbors, it burned to the ground. There was an eyewitness that claimed it was Matthew Patterson who started the fire. The eyewitness was Barton Turley, eldest son of Herb and Norlene Turley. The next day, at three o'clock in the afternoon, sheriff Tisdale came and arrested Matthew and took him to the office. The Turleys were there, and Barton swore that Mr. Patterson was the man he saw setting fire to the church. The next morning, a silver medal, engraved with a clover, had been found in the ashes of the church.

"We've got to have a hearing before the judge before I can hold him," the sheriff said.

"He needs to be put in jail," remarked Herb Turley.

"He's not going to flee, Turley, he owns the ferry," said the sheriff.

"Well when's the hearing," Norlene asked.

"Tomorrow morning, you'll have to be there," said the sheriff.

The next morning at nine o'clock Judge Jacobs opened the hearing. For several minutes the judge sat looking at the report the sheriff had written.

Judge Jacobs said, "Barton, it was in the dark of night when the fire was set, how can you be sure it was Mr. Patterson?"

"I recognized him. I know what he looks like," the boy replied.

"Couldn't you have been mistaken?" asked the judge, "It was dark. You do realize that false accusation is a crime."

"I'm sure it was him. Besides that, James Beasley found his medal in the ashes."

"How do you know it belongs to Mr. Patterson?" asked the judge.

"It's got a clover on it, everyone knows that," said Barton.

"Do you have such a medal, Mr. Patterson?" Judge Jacobs inquired.

"It is not my medal that was found. Mine is engraved with a shamrock," Matthew replied.

"Do you have it in your possession?" asked the judge.

"No, I don't sir, I gave it to someone," Matthew answered, "It would take a good deal of time to find it."

The judge said, "Mr. Patterson, I think you need to find it. But I don't think you need to be in custody."

"And why not?" asked Mr. Turley.

"Because, Mr. Turley, in the first place, he would have no motive for burning that church," said Judge Jacobs. "In the second place, he owns the ferry, and is obviously not going to go off and abandon it. Now I am the judge, and if you think you could do a better job why don't you run against me in the next election? Now, I'm going to allow Mr. Patterson two weeks to locate his medal, after which we'll set a trial date. Court is dismissed."

Judge Jacobs asked Matthew to stay behind for a few minutes. "About that medal, Matthew, when did you last see it?"

"When I got engaged to Ivory I gave to her. But then, when we got married I gave her a ring. So when Jimmy Sykes came back for the funeral, she gave it to him to bring him luck. I didn't think anything of it at the time, now this happened."

The judge said, "I have a pretty good idea who might have burned down the church and drummed up false evidence against you. This might be a good time to call on Mr. Hendricks. You're good friends aren't you? I wouldn't think it would be a good idea to send one of Jimmy's brothers."

"I agree," said Matthew, "Mitch is the best man to go, under the circumstances. Jimmy shouldn't be hard to locate, he stays close to the racetrack, I'm sure."

Mitchell Hendricks had heard about Matthew's problem and was on his way to the courthouse when he ran into him. "Keep the faith, sir," said Mitch.

Matthew said, "I think when I get up there and talk to God I'm going to ask him what he had in mind about this turn of events."

"I'm trying to think of how some good might come of it," said Mitch, "but I don't know either. I suggest we go talk to your in-laws."

They stopped at the livery stable to get the twins, then walked over to the Yellow House. When they arrived, Pearl and her two daughters were trying to console each other. "I know, baby, things feel bad, but they'll be better. Here's Mitch an' Matthew, I know they got a plan."

Mitch said, "Little Jim's got to be close to the fairground, he won't be hard to find."

"Lemme go wit' you," said Wendell, "he's my brother, I know I can find him."

Matthew said, "No, it's too dangerous for either of you, Mitch can find him as well as anybody."

Pearl said, "Mr. Hendricks, you a good, good man to do this, we be prayin' for you all the time."

"What else can you all tell me?" Mitch asked.

Ivory said, "He's been stayin' with Miss Velma at her eatin' place. He works for Johnny Moran sometimes. That's about all we know."

"That's fine, if he's in Hot Springs I'll find him."

Chester and Charles arrived at that point. "I got a horse you can ride, Mitch," said Chester, "his name's Blackbird. He's a hot-blooded horse and he's strong."

"Thank you, Chester," said Mitchell Hendricks, "that gives me everything I need. I'll go get some sleep and I'll be on my way."

Mitchell returned to Brother Davis' church. He went and talked to Eli Cotter. "Eli, I know it's a stretch of the imagination, but I might get hung up getting back here with Jimmy. I'm going to ask Jake Miles, if he sees me coming, to fire off his cannon. If you hear that cannon, start ringing the church bell, and keep ringing it until Little Jim or I get into town."

"My hearing isn't so good, Mitch, I don't know if I'll hear that gun from that far away," Eli said.

"Well, spread the word around, let everybody know to listen for it," said Mitch.

Mitch was up at the crack of dawn. He didn't want to lose any daylight on his journey. He stopped at the abode of of Gunner Jake. Jake was sitting on his front porch having his morning cup. "Good morning, it's Hendricks isn't it?"

"Yes, sir. I'd like to ask a favor," said Mitch.

"I'll oblige if I can," said Jake Miles.

"You may know they've accused Matthew Patterson of burning down the colored folks' church." said Mitch.

"Yes, I've heard about that."

"I'm on my way to Hot Springs to find Jimmy Sykes, so he can testify for Mr. Patterson. I don't know how long it will be before I come back, his trial is in two weeks. If you should see us, or if you have any clue that we'll be here soon, fire the cannon to let folks know we're on our way, can you do that?"

"Why, that Irishman is a hard worker and a help to the whole community, I'll be glad to do that," said Jake.

With that taken care of, he headed off towards the Sumacs. He thought about the times in the past when he had traveled up the Ouachita river. He'd never gone farther than Camden. As he rode north along the river he thought about this horse named Blackbird and Maj. Thornton, and Chester, who'd raised him. Chester must have thought he was a good horse for traveling or he wouldn't have put him in Mitch's care. When you're headed home from a trip, horses know their way. But when you're leaving home, they must have a different feeling altogether, maybe an unsettled feeling. He wished he could say to Blackbird that everything was under control, but he didn't feel that way himself. As he passed the Sumacs he knew there was no turning back, all he could do was keep riding. It was his love for Matthew, his faith in providence, and, above all, hope, that made him willing to do this.

It was the middle of the afternoon when he got to Camden. He found a stable and asked the man to give his horse some corn. The man said, "I'm Phillip Nunn. would that be one of Maj. Thornton's horses?"

"Yes, sir, this is Blackbird. It sounds crazy, but the ferryman in West Creek has been accused of arson, and I need to bring Little Jim Sykes back to testify on his behalf." Mitch explained.

"I remember Little Jim, he's been here several times. I'll take care of this horse. If you're hungry, go see Big Annie at her boarding house, she'll remember Big Jim and Little Jim."

Big Annie was very sympathetic to his plight. "Oh those selfish folks that want to tell the rest of us how to live, I'll take you to the kitchen and get Lunettie to fix you a plate." He debated with himself whether to spend the night there. He didn't feel tired, himself, but he knew Blackbird needed the rest. He was close to the town square so he walked in that direction. There was an oak tree by the courthouse that looked inviting so he sat down there. Matthew Patterson's troubles were going through his mind. The Turleys had a silver medal that they claimed was Matthew's. The Irishman knew it wasn't his. It was likely that the Turleys had gone to the expense of having a medal made somewhere so they could present it as their hard evidence. It was also very likely that a bigoted white person had set fire to the ABC;

hatred was all the motive they needed. But why Matthew? Well, he married a colored girl and that might be all the more reason to hate him, besides the fact that he was baptized Catholic. One could easily think that white southerners tended to embrace hatred, but he knew that there were white people in the north that wanted to keep Jews and Irish from entering the country. How long was it going to take for people to get over their prejudice?

Mitch walked back to the stable. Phil asked if he was going to stay the night.

"Oh, I guess I could stay at the hotel, but that would cost money, which I don't have a lot of," Mitch replied.

"Well, you could sleep in the hayloft, if you like." the man offered.

"If it's all right with you, I just might do that," said Mitch, "that way ol' Blackbird will get a good rest."

Mitch slept well in the hayloft. Maybe it was the nice weather or the smell of the open air, but his mind was at ease, he felt like he had good reason for everything he was doing.

In the morning he asked Phil if he was familiar with the road to Arkadelphia. "It's too far to ride in one day, you'll need to stop somewhere."

"What's a good place to stop?" asked Mitch.

"There's a lumber camp on the way there, they started calling it 'Gurdon', that's the one place I know of. Maj. Thornton's stayed there when he was going that way," said Phil.

"Thanks, that gives me someplace to plan for. Hope to see you in a week or so," Mitch replied.

The farther north he rode the less forest he saw. He saw vast fields of stumps, and it made him think that the timber must be worth a good deal of money for there to be so much of it cut. He had heard about Col. Fordyce and the railroads he was building. He guessed that this area must be expecting rail service, because how else could this timber be moved except by trains. Several times he asked passersby if he was coming to Gurdon. Some said they'd never heard of it, others just pointed north. He came to a crude toll bridge across a river that was less than half as wide as the Ouachita. Since it was the season of runoff it wasn't low enough to be forded. He rode up to the bridge and asked the toll collector what was the name of the stream. He was told it was the

Little Missouri river. He paid a nickel toll and rode across the bridge.

As sundown was approaching, Mitch saw what looked to be a settlement in the distance. There were wagons with teams of horses and mules, low buildings, and what looked to be a railway construction crew. As he drew closer he saw a sign on a building which read, 'The Concatenated Order of the Hoo-hoo'. He had no idea what this 'order' might be, but it seemed like a place where he could get information. He tied Blackbird to the hitching post and walked inside. There were chairs and tables with men sitting and reading newspapers, and drinking beer. He approached one of the tables and asked if there was a place he could board his horse overnight. One of the men asked, "What brings you here?"

Mitch replied, "I'm Mitchell Hendricks from West Creek, Arkansas and I'm on my way to Hot Springs to locate a certain person from my town."

A man from a table close by rose to his feet and asked, "Mr. Hendricks, did you say you are from West Creek?"

"Yes, sir, I am," Mitch replied.

"I'm Col. Lichtenberg, come sit down, please," he said. "Are you familiar with Maj. Thornton?"

"Yes, I am. He passed away recently, you know," said Mitch. "

"Yes, I know, who is the person you're looking for?" asked the colonel.

"I'm looking for a negro named Little Jim Sykes," said Mitch.

"He's not in Hot Springs, you know."

"Oh, do you know where he is?"

"He is working for a man named Prothro, who has a mining claim near the headwaters of the Little Missouri river."

"That's the river I crossed today."

"Ah, why do you need to find Jim Sykes?"

"An Irish ferryman in West Fork has been falsely accused of arson. Little Jim is his brother-in-law, and he needs him to testify on his behalf in court."

"I see. Well, to find him, you need to follow the Little Missouri upstream. I've never been there myself, but I understand that the land is quite hilly. It rises fairly steeply as you travel west. I'm told there is a very wide flat area just before you come to the gorge in which Mr. Prothro is mining. But wait 'til tomorrow to start, come to my house and spend the night, and then start in the morning."

Col. Lichtenberg had Mitch put his horse in the corral with his own horses and had him sit down to supper with his family. "What is the reason for this false accusation in West Creek?" the colonel wanted to know.

"Well, I'll tell you the facts," said Mitch, "you can draw your own conclusions. This Irishman, named Matthew Patterson, built a ferry by the Ouachita river. I've helped him from time to time, and he's helped me. He married Jimmy's sister. Just recently someone set fire to the Abyssinian Baptist Church. Several white people say they found a silver medal, belonging to Matthew, in the ashes of the fire. We know it isn't Matthew's medal, his was given to Little Jim several years ago. That's why I need to find Jimmy and bring him back before the trial."

Col. Lichtenberg nodded. "It sounds like these people have a resentment for an Irish Catholic who married into a colored family."

"My feelings exactly," Mitch replied.

"Well it's highly commendable of you to make this journey to help your friend," said the colonel, "You get some sleep and set off in the morning. And if there is anything I can help you with don't hesitate to ask."

"You've been very helpful already," said Mitch, "I can't tell you how much I appreciate it."

Mitch slept on the couch in the colonel's parlor. Right after breakfast he bid goodbye to Col. Lichtenberg and his family and went in search of the Little Missouri. He assumed that people from Saint Louis, or near there, named the river. It branched off from the Ouachita at the same angle that the Missouri branched off from the Mississippi.

There wasn't much of a trail in that direction and he rode for at least five miles before he could see the slope of the valley that showed him he was following the river. The ground was rough and rocky and was wooded with evergreens mixed with hardwood. By this time he could see no sign of human habitation. He thought it must look very much the same as it did before European explorers came there. Now he would have to find grazing for Blackbird and shelter for himself. He could only pray that Little Jim and this Welshman were still staying in the same place he had been told they were. It was slow going, this process of traveling up the river without winding along the riverbank, which could take a crucially long time to get anywhere. When he came upon a patch of grass or broad leaf growth of any kind, he stopped and let the horse graze for a while.

The water looked fresh and clear, so he drank from it when he was thirsty. He tried not ponder over how much animal or human waste was carried in the stream. He had with him some dried meat and hard biscuits which he forced down when he got really hungry. He hadn't planned on being so far from human habitation, and it looked as though it would be many days without seeing food which was prepared in a kitchen. When it got dark he looked for a sheltered place, like a rock out-cropping or a wide hardwood tree. He would tether the horse on a long line so he could graze as much as possible. He noticed the croak of bull frogs one evening. He made a crude spear by sharpening a stick with his knife. Building a small fire he roasted the frogs legs. It was the best meal he'd had in three days.

  For eight nights and eight days he worked his way up the steep banks of the winding river. Finally the steep banks gave way to a gradual slope. By the time he had gone another half mile there was a wide, level area that spread for miles. It had to be the flat area Col. Lichtenberg mentioned. Off in the distance he could see more hills. The river appeared to be following its edge of the level area. He decided to ride straight across toward the hills. There was lush grassy vegetation. He dismounted and took the bridle off Blackbird. He loosened the saddle girth and let him graze. He seemed to relish the tall grass. The area looked like the most tillable land he had seen since he left West Fork. After traveling three or four miles he was across the level area and into the hills. The riverbanks grew steep again. He had the feeling he must be near his destination. It was slow going, as he had to stay right by the river's edge in order to travel upstream. The footing was too unstable for the horse so Mitch dismounted and led him. For the next six hours he followed the stream.

 Then he smelled the pungency of pine smoke. He knew if it was a campfire it must be close to the riverbank, so he kept plodding away until, finally, he saw the camp. There was a tall white man close by. He called out, "Sir, are you Mr. Prothro?"

"Might I know who *you* are," the man replied.

"I'm Mitchell Hendricks from West Creek," Mitch replied.

"And what brings you here?"

"I'm looking for a negro boy named Jimmy Sykes."

"I'm alone here, I don't know anyone that fits that description. Why do you seek this person?"

"A mutual friend of ours is on trial for a crime he didn't commit. Jim is the only person who could save him."

"How do I know any of this is true?"

From a short distance away, a voice said,"It's all right, Mr. Prothro, I know this man. He lives in my hometown."

Little Jim soon came into view. Mitch said, "Thank God," as he smiled. "How are you Jimmy?"

"I'm good, how are you Mr. Mitch?" Little Jim asked.

"Very tired, I've been riding for nine days now."

Jimmy said, "Mr. Prothro, this is Mr. Hendricks, I been knowin' him for years."

Mr. Prothro said, "If what you say is true, I'd say the accused man has a very good friend to come all this way to help him."

Mitch asked, "Well Jim, will you come with me to West Creek?"

Mr. Prothro said, "You may go with him with my blessing, this ore's been in the ground for thousands of years, it will still be here another week or so."

Mitch tied Blackbird with a long rope under a tree where he had plenty of grass. "You don't mind if I lie down a while, do you?" he asked.

"You go right ahead," said Jimmy, "I know you're tired."

After a good night's rest, Jim and Mitch were on their way. The one good aspect of the trip was that now they were going downhill. Blackbird and Sparrow had both come from Maj. Thornton's herd. You couldn't argue that they weren't first-rate riding horses, and even better, they'd never been abused.

"They's fish in this river, Mr. Mitch," said Little Jim.

"Yes, I know," Mitch replied, "the Caddo people who lived here had plenty of fish and game to eat, besides berries and nuts. I think they lived pretty well here."

"What one man can eat, any other man can eat too," Jimmy replied.

"You do have Matthew's medal don't you? I just remembered I never asked you that," said Mitch.

"I sure do," Jimmy answered, "I never thought too much about it 'til you came and told me he was in trouble. Then I thought, why did I run off with this thing, I didn't need it."

"Well, who would have thought this would happen?" said Mitch.

"We don't know," Little Jim remarked, "maybe there's some reason for all this."

"That's the same thing I said to Matthew before I left town. But neither of us could say what that reason might be," Mitch replied, "we'll just wait and see."

As the incline lessened they didn't have to stay so close to the riverbank and they could make more progress. They thought about crossing to the southern side of the stream but since they knew that they could get to the Ouachita the way they were going, why take a chance. When it came time to stop and spend the night, Mitch felt less worried about their time schedule. He had been gone for nine days, and the judge had said the trial would start in two weeks. The judge also said that the trial would last two or more days, and because of some legal questions he didn't quite understand, there might be more of a delay. If he'd known how long it would take to find Jimmy he would have asked for more time. But that was all in the past now, they were on their way. They could only hope that they wouldn't have any delays.

Chapter 33

Back in West Creek, Judge Jacobs had discussed the coming trial with a judge in a neighboring county, a Judge Peterson. They had decided that to properly carry out the proceedings, they needed an attorney to represent Matthew Patterson and they needed someone to preside besides Judge Jacobs. Judge Peterson agreed to come to West Creek and sit for the trial. This made it necessary to delay the trial another day. Judge Jacobs asked Seth Tate to represent Matthew. Mr. Tate said that he didn't know anything about a court trial. "You don't need to, Seth, I'll write down all the things you need know to do the job. Nobody's going to care if you read it from a sheet of paper. You'll do fine."

They had asked the clerk of Ouachita Co., a Mr. Turner, to prosecute the case against Matthew. Mr. Patterson's accusers didn't object to that arrangement. They didn't even know they could object. If everything went as planned, Judge Jacobs knew they shouldn't have a problem. The only question was, whether or not Jimmy Sykes would be there to testify.

Judge Jacobs sent word to Matthew to meet him at Sheriff Tisdale's office. When Matthew got there, the judge asked him to sit down. "Now, Matthew, the trial's going to start in three days. I'm going to ask you, that for the course of the trial, you stay here with the sheriff, in his office."

"Well, if it's necessary, I will," Matthew responded.

"Well, for the appearance of propriety, I think we have to. In the meantime, you're free to go about your affairs. Just don't leave town," said the judge.

After Matthew had left, Mr. Beasley and Mr. Turley came in the sheriff's office. "You ain't gonna leave him locked up?" Mr King asked.

"No, he's innocent until proven guilty," the judge replied.

Mr. Turley said, "Huh, yore gonna have a hard time provin' he's innocent."

"No, Mr. Turley, nobody has to prove he's innocent. You have to prove he's guilty."

After Messrs Beasley and Turley had left, Sheriff Tisdale asked the judge, "What will you do for a jury for the trial?"

"They haven't asked for a jury trial. It's usually the defendant in a case that requests a jury, and Mr. Patterson obviously doesn't want a jury," the judge replied. "If we were going to actually seat a jury, it would have to be made up of people who aren't acquainted with any of the people involved. That would be hard to do in a town this size."

Continuing down the Little Missouri, Mitch and Little Jim were hoping the weather would stay clear, at least until they reached the Ouachita. There were stretches where they dismounted and led their horses when there were rocks or soft places that made the footing unsteady. Mitch felt like Little Jim could handle horses in a way few humans could. He never tried to force them to do anything. He simply let them know where he wanted them to go and let them take their own time in doing it. He made it look so easy, but he could also get a horse to run at the limit of its ability. Mitch knew that he could never forget this little man and wanted to help him and his family any way he could.

The ground was gradually less steep as they came out of the hills. By the following morning they were in sight of the Ouachita river. After resting a while and letting the horses graze, they proceeded toward the toll bridge. It soon became apparent that Blackbird was spooked at the sight of the bridge. He was breathing heavily and tossing his head.

"I wonder what's wrong with him," Mitch asked.

"Step down a minute, sir," Jimmy said softly.

Mitch dismounted. "Hand me the reins," Jimmy said. Mitch handed him the reins. Little Jim was talking to him very softly. "Easy boy, what's wrong? Easy, just be easy." Then he said, "He came across here before, but he's mixed up, like he thinks he's goin' somewhere he don't like. You take Sparrow an' walk across ahead 'o' me. I'll walk him across after you."

Mitch paid their tolls and then led Sparrow onto the bridge. He went slowly. Looking back over his shoulder he saw Little Jim with his head next to Blackbird's talking to him as he led him slowly across. Halfway across Blackbird seemed to relax, and walked on across the bridge.

"How do you do that, Jim?" Mitch wanted to know.

Jimmy smiled, "You just remember some time when you was little and you was scared and you know how he feels."

Now all they had to do was follow this river road back through Camden and the Sumacs and on home. But would they make it in time? It was the fourteenth day since Mitch had left West Fork. He felt like they needed to hurry, but he had felt like that the whole time since he started. The fact was that these horses were tired. Because of them being pushed along, they really hadn't had a good long rest.

Chapter 34

Matthew was getting despondent about having to sit in the jail cell overnight. The food came from the hotel kitchen where Clothilda did her best to fix the things he liked best. Breakfast was fried eggs and grits with biscuits and hot coffee. She always sent him a big dinner, but he found he was losing his usual appetite. Too many things were going around in his head. Maybe Mitch couldn't find Jim. Maybe He'd lost the medal. Ivory came and visited with him twice a day, and sat in court with her whole family every minute of the trial. But he couldn't sleep at all. He kept asking himself, "Why is this happening to me?"

Judge Peterson had read the charges being brought against Matthew. After the formalities, Mr. Turner called Barton Turley to witness. "Mr. Turley, did you see the defendant set fire to the Abyssinian Baptist Church on the night of April the fourteenth?"

Barton: "Ah, who?"

Turner: "The defendant, Mr. Patterson."

Barton: "Yes, I did."

Turner: "How did you know it was Mr. Patterson?"

Barton: "I, ah, seen him before."

Turner: "You have seen him where?"

Barton: "At the ferry, he runs the ferry."

Turner: "All right, Mr. Tate, your witness."

Seth Tate had a sheet of paper in his hand with every possible question there was about Barton Turley's witnessing of the crime. Which side of the church was he on, how dark was it, how far away was Patterson, what did he do when he saw the fire, why didn't he call for help, why was he out at that place at that time. The strategy was to get him to talk long enough to contradict himself. But when it came right down to it, it was his word against the word of someone else.

Then it was James Beasley in the witness chair.

Turner: "What evidence can you bring forward?"

Beasley: "I found the Irishman's medal in the ashes the next morning."

Turner: "I assume you mean the defendant."

Beasley: "Patterson."

Turner: "How did you know it was his medal?"

Beasley: "It has a clover on it. Everybody knows he has a

medal with a clover on it."

Turner: "I see. Mr. Tate has some questions."

Mr. Tate asked, "Do you have this medal in your possession?" James Beasley withdrew the medal from his pocket and handed it to Mr. Tate.

Tate: "Very well, let's put this medal on the judge's table as an exhibit."

Then it was Matthew's turn to testify.

Turner: "Mr. Patterson, where were you on the night of April fifteenth?"

Matthew: "I was at home in bed."

Turner: "All night?"

Matthew: "Yes, all night."

Turner: "Did anyone else know you were there?"

Matthew: "Yes, my wife, Ivory."

Turner: "Are you aware of the medal Mr. Beasley says he found in the ashes?"

Matthew: "'Tis not my medal. I gave mine to my wife, then she gave it to her brother, Jimmy Sykes.
If you wait 'til he gets here you can see it for yourself."

Turner said, "All right Mr. Tate, you may question the witness.

Tate: "Mr. Patterson, where was this medal made?"

Matthew: "In Ireland."

Tate: "What can you tell me about it?"

Matthew: "'Tis made from an Irish half crown and has a shamrock carved on it."

Tate: "Did you set fire to the Abyssinian Baptist Church?"

Matthew: "I did not. I would never set fire to any church or any other building, I would have no reason to."

David Thornton and his wife Camilla were in the back of the courtroom when Camilla asked David to step outside with her.

"David, do you know which road into town Mitch and Jimmy will be taking?" she asked.

"The road north along the river," he replied.

"Their horses will be exhausted from their long trip. Why don't we take some horses and start riding north, we're bound to run into them if they're coming from that direction," she suggested.

"Well, all right, I don't see what harm it could do," David answered. They mounted up and headed for Darley Hill.

As they came riding up through the gate, Chester came out

to meet them.

"Chester, put halters on Angel and Falcon," David said, "and water them. We're going out to meet up with Jimmy and Mitchell with fresh horses for them to ride."

David and Camilla each took a lead rope in hand and rode down through the Darley Hill gate; Camilla leading Angel and David leading Falcon. They rode north along the river, heading for the Sumacs. They broke into a gentle lope, Camilla in front, David behind. They were both thinking, "I hope the boys aren't too far away." But they knew that the farther they rode, the sooner they would meet up with Jimmy and Mitch. As they rode past Gunner Jake's house they saw him standing on his front porch waving as they went by. They stayed at their gentle pace. Before long they were approaching the Sumacs. When they got there, Camilla raised up her hand and reined in her horse.
David trotted up alongside her.

"Let's let them catch their breath," said Camilla, "we don't want to tire them out too much."

"All right," David answered, "we'll stop every few miles, I have a hunch they're not far off."

Mitchell Hendricks was so tired he was seeing spots in front of his eyes. It all seemed like a dream. He was thinking that when this was all over with, no one could say that he and Jimmy hadn't done their level best to get back and help their friend; and that included these two horses that the major had produced. "How do you feel, Jim?" he asked.

"I can't feel nothin'," Little Jim replied, "let's slow down for a minute." They slowed to a trot and then to a walk. It seemed like they had just passed Camden, but they knew it was at least six hours.

"Wait," Jimmy cried, "look up there. I see horses coming." They broke into a trot once more, then to a lope.

Mitch said, "Somebody's coming, it looks like three or four horses- it's four horses."

In a few minutes David and Camilla rode up to them. Jimmy cried, "Oh Lord, it looks like the Redbird done turned back into a colt."

"It's his son, Alizarin Angel. We thought you fellows could use some fresh horses," said Camilla.

Little Jim jumped to the ground. "Is the trial still goin'?" he asked.

"It was when we left this morning," David replied.

Jim was loosening the cinch on Sparrow. "Help me get this saddle on that big red horse. Boy, I hope you feel like runnin' 'cause that's what we gonna do."

They boosted Jimmy up on Angel's back. "You go on ahead, Jim, I'll be right along," yelled Mitch.

Angel thundered off down the river road. It seemed to Jimmy that the colt sensed the urgency of the situation. That was fine because there was no time to waste. The colt was in almost a dead run as they approached the Sumacs. Angel seemed to have a fire burning inside him as they passed the Sumacs and curved slightly east toward West Creek. He could see Gunner Jake's house up ahead. Then he realized Jake was waving his hands over his head for Jimmy to slow down. He reined Angel in and slowed him to a trot.

"Get down and hold him," Jake called out, "I'm fixin' to fire my cannon."

Little Jim asked no questions, and did what the man said. Jake Miles jogged to the back of his house. He bent over his field piece while he struck a match. "Kaboom!" the gun went off like a thunderclap.

Jimmy led Angel over to Jake's porch and climbed into the saddle. In seconds he was in full stride, riding towards town.

"Clang, clang, clang clang..." went the bell on the Methodist church. Eli Cotter kept pulling on the rope with no intention of stopping until he was made to.

People all over town and inside the courtroom were looking up in bewilderment.

Judge Peterson started pounding his gavel on the table top as he called out, "Until I find out what is going on, this court will be in recess."

Jimmy slowed to a trot and rode up to the porch of the hotel. The bell was still clanging and people were shouting all around the courtroom. "It's Little Jim, he's here, he's here..." children were shouting.

Someone finally got to Eli and told him it was all right, he could stop ringing the bell.

Little Jim's brothers took hold of Angel's reins and led him over to Ira's stable. Mitch Hendricks soon galloped into town and likewise headed for the stable. An hour had gone by before calm drifted over West Creek and the court proceedings were resumed.

Little Jim Sykes was asked to sit in the witness chair. The judge said, "Before we go any further, Jim Sykes, do have in your possession a medal that once belonged to Mr. Matthew Patterson? If so, may I see it?" Jimmy handed him the medal.

"I will mark this exhibit 'B', and I am placing it alongside the other medal which is exhibit 'A'. Anyone who wishes may come forward, one at a time and look at the two exhibits. Several people stood in line and looked at the two medals lying on the table.

The judge said, "Jim Sykes you may sit with your family. Mr. Patterson, will you examine the two medals on the table." Matthew rose and walked to the table and looked at the medals. "Is one of these the medal which you gave Mrs. Patterson who then gave it to Jim Sykes?"

"Yes, your honor, exhibit 'B' is the one. Exhibit 'A' is a four-leaf-clover; mine is a shamrock- a three-leaf-clover."

"Thank you, Mr. Patterson, you may sit down," said Judge Peterson, "Does anyone in the courtroom have an argument with Mr. Patterson over which medal is his?" No one in the courtroom spoke. "Seeing none, I shall rule that the accusation against Matthew Patterson is wholly without merit and he is free to go. I also rule that someone has deliberately misled the court by counterfeiting a piece of evidence with the purpose of making a false accusation. This matter will be under continuing investigation by the jurisdiction of this town and this county. Court is adjourned."

Judge Peterson tapped his gavel on the table.
There were shouts, and there were groans and there were whistles, and the bell started ringing again. This time it wasn't Eli, but Mitch Hendricks that was pulling on the rope.

Matthew Patterson and Miss Pearl's family were standing out in front of the hotel with lots of hugging and blessing going on. A small black boy was tugging on Jimmy's sleeve. "What you want, child?" Jim asked.

"Is you got any children, Little Jim?" the boy asked.

"No, I'm just a single man," Jimmy replied.

"I ain't got no daddy, Little Jim, you could be my daddy," the boy replied.

"Maybe I could, I don't know, "Jimmy replied, "I got to go back up the river for a few weeks before I can come back."

Miss Pearl said, "Come here child, you got a place to stay as long as you need." She picked the boy up.
"We'll talk to your mama, every child around here has a family, and that means you, too."

Cover Art:

The painting on the cover of this book was made by Shae
Maranna House. Born in Camden, Arkansas, she studied
painting at University of Arkansas at Little Rock where she
earned her Bachelor of Fine Art degree. She has been
involved in community art projects in Little Rock, and works
as a portrait painter. Shae currently resides in Paron,
Arkansas in the foothills of the Ouachita Mountains with her
husband and two boys.

www.ingramcontent.com/pod-product-compliance
Lightning Source LLC
Chambersburg PA
CBHW081208170626
46811CB00010B/3227